SUPER #1
GOOFBALLS
that Stinking Feeling

SUPER GOOFBALLS

Book One: That Stinking Feeling

Book Two: Goofballs in Paradise

SUPER GOOFBALLS #1
that Stinking Feeling

written and illustrated by
peter Hannan

HarperTrophy®
An Imprint of HarperCollinsPublishers

This book is dedicated to Dru. The words, pictures, and punctuation are all dedicated to Dru. The page numbers? Dru. The barcode and binding? Dru and Dru. Even this dedication is dedicated to Dru.

Super Goofballs, Book 1: That Stinking Feeling
Copyright © 2007 by Peter Hannan
All rights reserved. Printed in the United States of America.
No part of this book may be used or reproduced in any manner whatsoever without written permission except in the case of brief quotations embodied in critical articles and reviews. For information address HarperCollins Children's Books, a division of HarperCollins Publishers, 1350 Avenue of the Americas, New York, NY 10019.
www.harpercollinschildrens.com

Library of Congress Cataloging-in-Publication Data
Hannan, Peter.
    That stinking feeling / Peter Hannan.—1st ed.
        p.   cm.— (Super goofballs ; bk. 1)
    Summary: When superhero Amazing Techno Dude and his grandmother, the Bodacious Backwards Woman, take in several zany roommates, it is the zanies who come to the rescue when Fabian the Fabulous Flatulent Fiend threatens to unleash his superpowers on the city.
    ISBN-10: 0-06-085212-7 (trade bdg.)
    ISBN-13: 978-0-06-085212-2 (trade bdg.)
    ISBN-10: 0-06-085211-9 (pbk.)
    ISBN-13: 978-0-06-085211-5 (pbk.)
    [1. Heroes—Fiction. 2. Humorous stories.] I. Title.
PZ7.H1978Th 2007   2006016539
[Fic]—dc22   CIP
                                                                      AC

Typography by Joel Tippie
❖
First Harper Trophy edition, 2007

TABLE OF CONTENTS

CHAPTER 1:
The Shrieking Stinkbug of Stench

I smelled her before I saw her. I don't have super-smelling powers or anything. She just really stinks. Queen Smellina the Shrieking Stinkbug of Stench is a very smelly, very evil, very insane flying-insect–supervillain lady. Number one on the Slimy Sleazeball Superchart for 137 weeks in a row.

Hovering six stories above us, surrounded by a vomit-green haze, her outstretched wings cast a shadow over Gritty City City Hall.

The queen smiled a huge, superloony smile and screamed. Her voice was as horrible as her stench.

"GOOD MORNING, STUPID HEROES!"

"Good 'til you stunk it up!" I yelled back.

"Stinkypants Miss Little, yeah!" yelled Granny the Bodacious Backwards Woman. She says and does everything backwards.

Queen Smellina arched her back *way* back and sucked in an enormous breath. I could feel the suction on my face. One of my gloves ripped off and flew into her mouth. Followed by my shoes, socks, and the other glove. And Granny's teeth.

Queen Smellina froze like an ugly floating statue for a few seconds. Then she lunged forward and hacked a huge horrible hurl of her Hyper-Bad Breath Ray right at us.

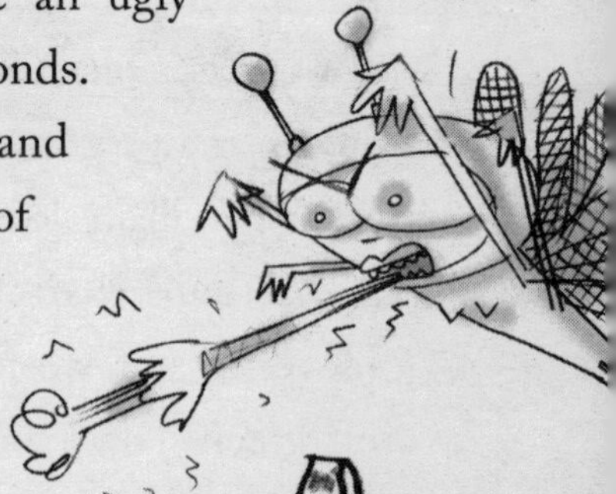

"HA-HA-HA-HA-HHHHAAACKKKKK!!!!!!"

"Stenchfire! Incoming!" I shouted, diving hard to the right. The hot, glowing stench burned my eyebrows. I whipped around in time

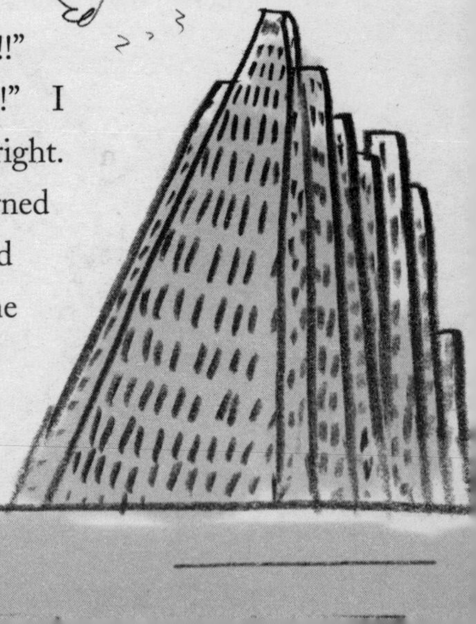

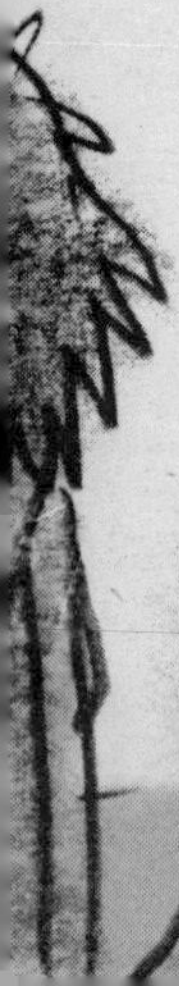

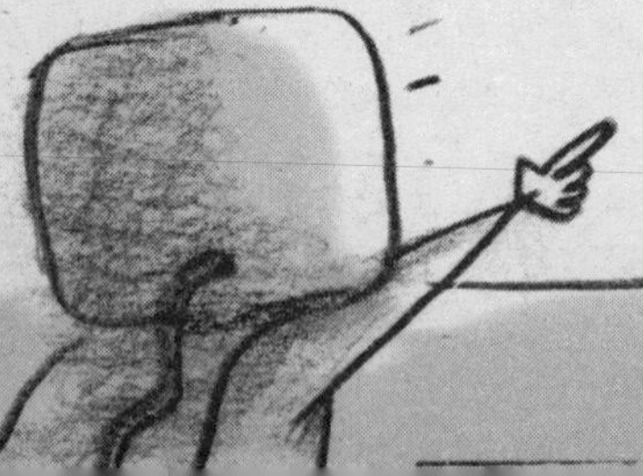

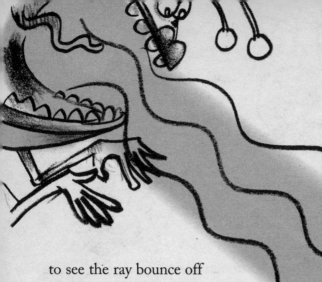

to see the ray bounce off
of five skyscrapers and out
over Gritty City Harbor.

"There's a lot more where that came
from, idiot-box boy!"

"Lady insect stinky, trap your shut!" yelled
Granny.

"You wish, you butt-backwards old biddy!" she said
before hacking again: "HA-HA-HA-HA-HA-
HHHHHAAACKKKKK!!!"

Her stench hit me like an atomic stink bomb. The
screen of my Amazing Techno Dude Deluxe TV
Helmet shattered, and I inhaled a massive dose of
blistering disgustingness.

"I think you stink!" I gagged.

3

"Stink you *know* I!" gagged Granny.

"WELL, STANK YOU VERY MUCH!" Smellina cackled. "YOU GET IT? *STANK* INSTEAD OF *THANK*? HEE, HEE, HEE, HEE, HEE! I CRACK ME UP!"

She always explains her jokes. As if they're hard to understand. Any five-year-old could make a joke like that. Five-year-olds don't usually hack deadly bad-breath rays though.

Smellina unleashed yet another blast. Granny and I dove into a Dumpster as the ray slammed into its side. I reached into my holster for my Amazing Techno Dude Handheld Remote, punched in the secret code, and hit Enter. Then I crossed my fingers.

But nothing happened. Queen Smellina looked down at us and smiled her evil smile.

"LOOKS LIKE IT'S TIME TO TAKE OUT

THE TRASH! HA, HA, HEE, HEE, HA!" Then her laugh turned into a shriek. This is her trademark. It meant she was about to finish us off with one final hack of horribleness.

"SHRIEK! SHRIEK! SHRIEK! SHHHH-HHRRRRRRRRIEEEEEEEEEEK . . . !!!"

We were goners.

But wait! A huge male flying insect appeared from around the corner of Gritty City City Bank. He looked like a gigantic insect movie star—very muscle-bound, very handsome—well, you know, for an insect.

He flashed a loverboy smile and spoke in a super-low, romantic voice. Strangely, he put accents on the wrong syllables.

"GreeTINGS, queeNIE-pie. HunKY ValENtine here. AND I am IN LOVE." Except he stretched out "love" for about ten seconds: "LOOOOOOOOOOOOO-OOOOVE."

He wiggled his fingers at her, doing one of those corny love waves.

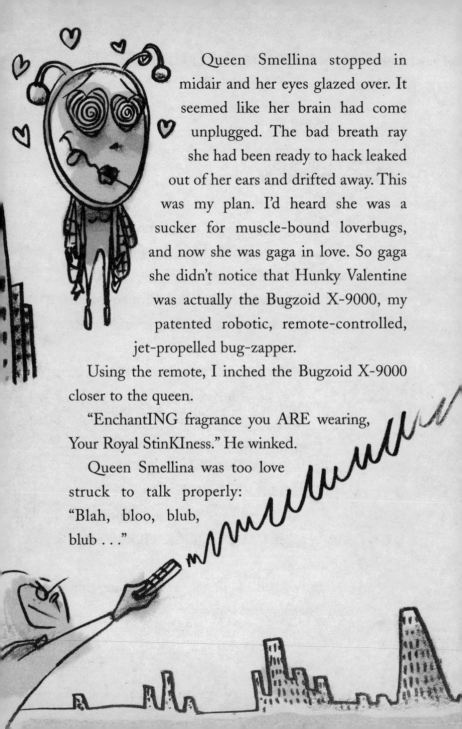

Queen Smellina stopped in midair and her eyes glazed over. It seemed like her brain had come unplugged. The bad breath ray she had been ready to hack leaked out of her ears and drifted away. This was my plan. I'd heard she was a sucker for muscle-bound loverbugs, and now she was gaga in love. So gaga she didn't notice that Hunky Valentine was actually the Bugzoid X-9000, my patented robotic, remote-controlled, jet-propelled bug-zapper.

Using the remote, I inched the Bugzoid X-9000 closer to the queen.

"EnchantING fragrance you ARE wearing, Your Royal StinKIness." He winked.

Queen Smellina was too love struck to talk properly: "Blah, bloo, blub, blub . . ."

"BeauTIful, smelLY, and *such* A way WITH words," purred the robot.

"Gloob goo, boo, boo . . ."

"Ooooo! HunKY love baBY-talk. How 'bout a big kisSY-wisSY?"

This was getting sickening, but it was working.

I moved the Bugzoid's

hunky lips even closer and puckered them up.

Smellina closed her eyes and finally found the words: "Hunky—you fascinating fellow you—kiss me!"

"okIE-dokIE," said Hunky, and boy, what a kiss. One touch of my Electro-Lip-Lock Smoocher-Zapper button and it was all over. The Bugzoid's mechanical lips clenched Queen Smellina's in a hyper-vise-grip and zapped her. She tried to scream, but since her lips were locked tight, she just hummed a great buzz of pain. She sounded like a sick rat with a kazoo in its mouth.

Then the Bugzoid X-9000's robotic arms squeezed her in an industrial-strength hug-lock. The lip-lock/hug-lock combo always works. This battle was over.

And boy, was I glad. The Hyper-Bad Breath Ray is icky beyond belief. It's a miracle that Granny and I survived with mere third-degree stench burns and an inability to eat solid food for a month. It was more than worth it, though, to see the freaky-funny look on Queen Smellina's face as Hunky Valentine hauled her off to jail.

She growled as only a crazy bug lady can. She was *so* mad, saying, "I AM SOOOOO MAD! AND I DON'T JUST

MEAN MAD-CRAZY, EVEN THOUGH I'M WELL KNOWN FOR THAT! AND I PROMISE THAT ONE DAY I'LL GET YOU, YOU UN-SUPER BLANKETY-BLANKS!!!!"

"Wow . . . maybe you're *angry* because you're *embarrassed* about falling in love with a fake mechanical insect," I replied. "I mean, didn't you notice that his head was held on with duct tape and his eyes were ordinary light bulbs?"

"BUT SUCH DREAMY LIGHT BULBS!!!" she cried.

How could a superevil mastermind such as Queen Smellina be so darn stupid? Well, love is stupid. No, that's not it. Love is blind. Or at least it has very blurred vision.

CHAPTER 2:
Always Thanking

Mayor What's-His-Name held a big ceremony in the park to thank us.

"With deepest gratitude, I, the Honorable Mayor What's-His-Name, hereby present the Bodacious Backwards Woman and her cute and spunky little sidekick with another terrific trophy for their mantel! Boy, it sure would be super if our super duo said a few words! Perhaps they'll thank us for thanking them again!" The crowd went wild. Everyone was smiling gigantic smiles. Everyone but me. I stepped up to the microphone.

"Yes . . . how nice. Another trophy for our mantel. Make that *mantels*. We just keep buying mantels. We've got medals and trophies on mantels in every room in the house! Floor to stupid ceiling! You would

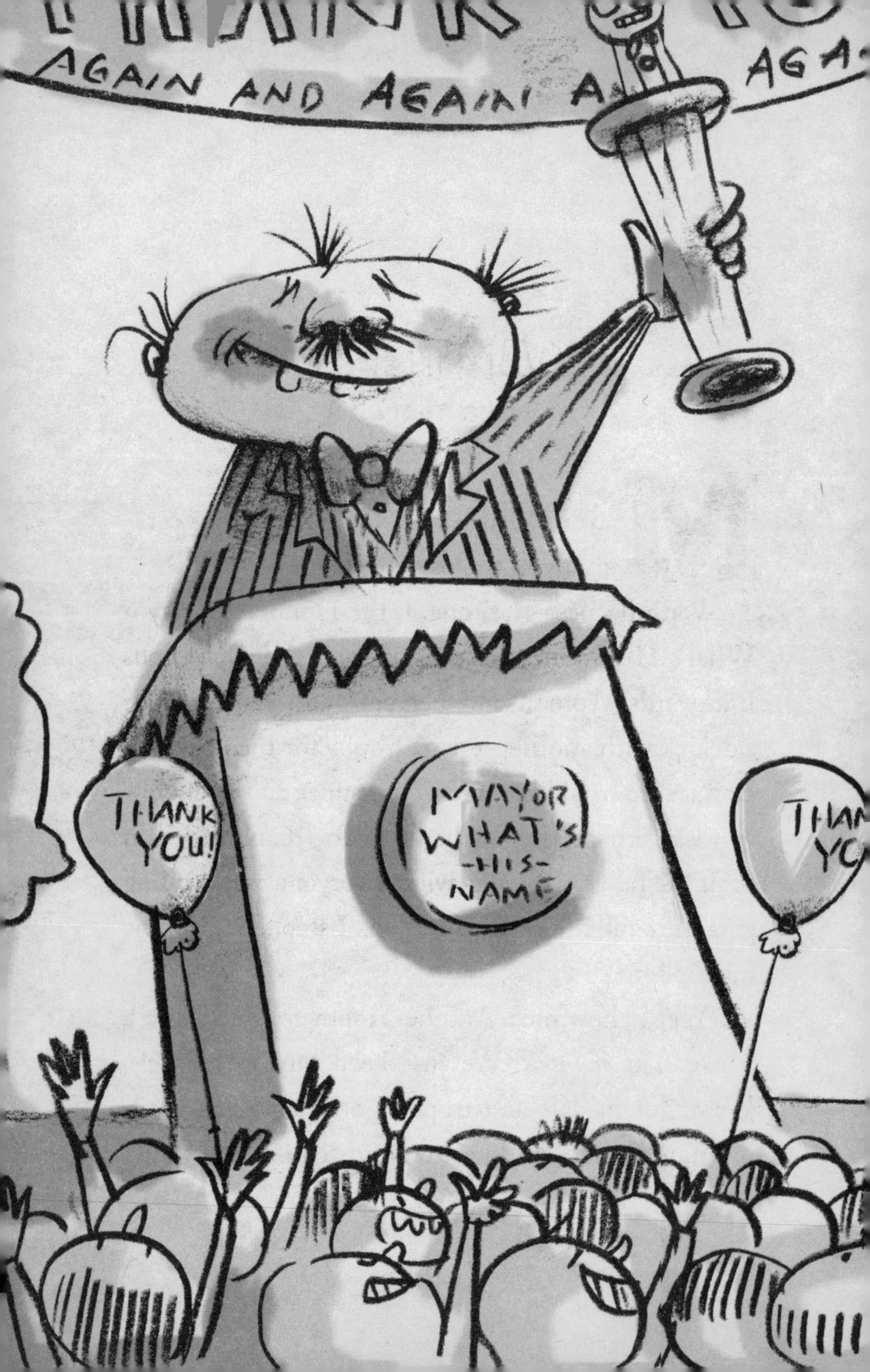
AGAIN AND AGAIN A
AGA
THANK YOU!
MAYOR WHAT'S -HIS- NAME
THAN YO

not believe how much money we spend on mantels. And since this trophy is a nice big one, we'll need one of those nice, big, expensive mantels. And you probably don't know this, but superheroes don't have a lot of money, because—news flash—we don't get paid! Sure, we get freebies from you citizens, and don't think we don't appreciate them, but how many day-old doughnuts can somebody eat? Meanwhile, I desperately need gadgets, but our gadget budget has been totally blown on mantels we never wanted in the first place. So, thanks a whole heck of a lot, and I'll catch you later because I've gotta go mantel shopping. Oh, and one more thing: if I hear anyone say 'cute and spunky little sidekick' one more time, I swear I'm using my powers for evil!"

The crowd was a lot quieter now.

Until Granny walked backwards to the microphone and said in her sweetest granny voice, "People wonderful, wonderful you, much very you thank!"

Once they figured out what the heck she'd said, the crowd went wild again.

Then Mayor What's-His-Name told us about how prison has made Queen Smellina more wicked and wacko than ever. She's obsessed with Granny and me: cursing, calling us names, perfecting her Hyper-Bad-Breath Ray through long hours of target practice (using a picture of us—with pimples drawn on and teeth blacked out—as the target), and screaming for revenge from the confines of her maximum-security misery.

"But don't worry, son," the Mayor said, patting me on the head. "They locked her up and threw away the key."

CHAPTER 3:

Granny and Me

This Thursday just plain started out bad. At exactly 6:03 A.M., the chimney collapsed, the toilet exploded, and the doorbell caught fire. It didn't occur to me, while dodging bricks, flames, and raw sewage, that these were merely the first three disasters of a very long weekend of disasters. But I'm getting ahead of myself.

The Bodacious Backwards Woman is at least a hundred and eight years old. She isn't my actual granny, but she's the only family I've got. She found me glued to a TV on her front step when I was an infant. And I mean literally glued to a TV. There are many weird theories about this. Some say I was raised by wild TVs.

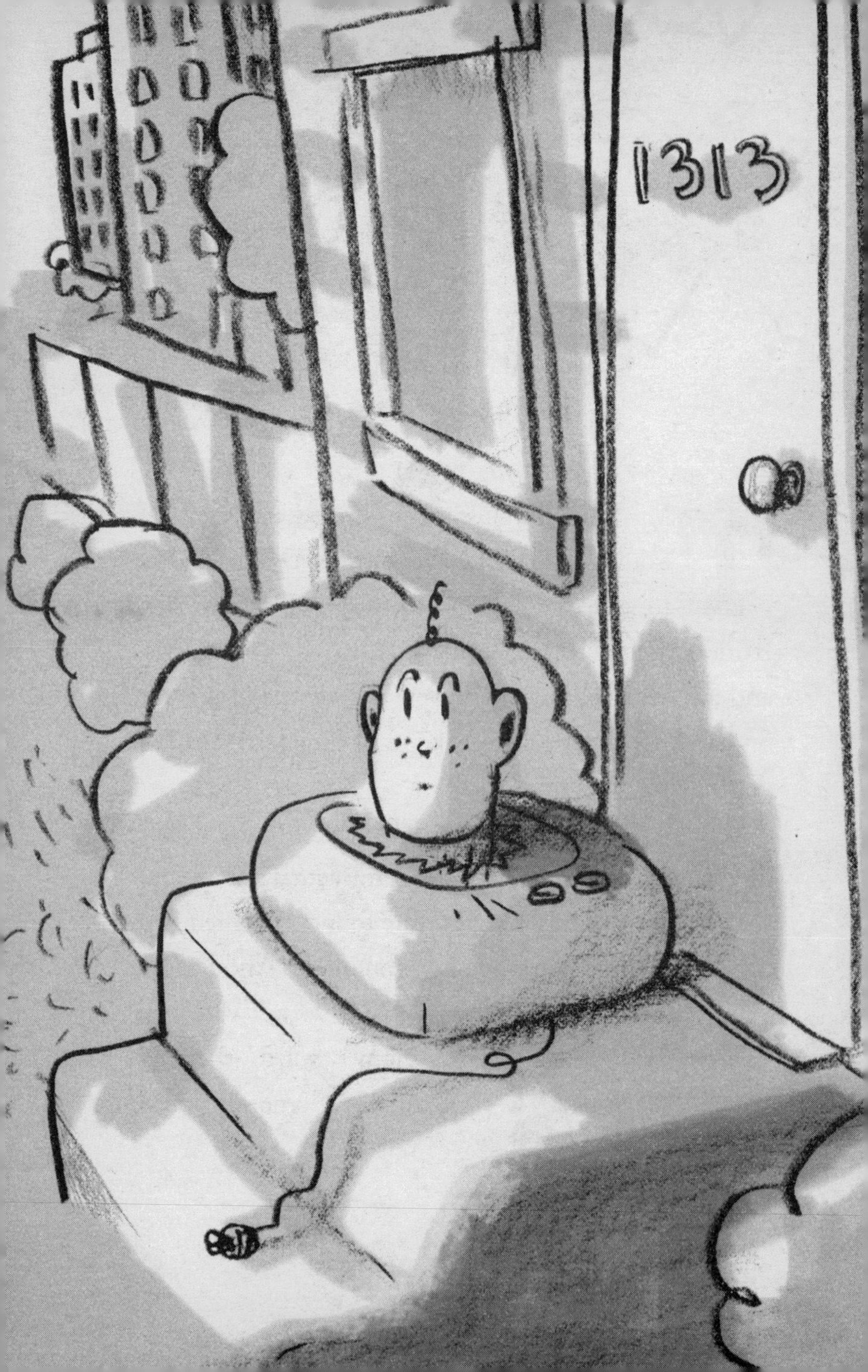
1313

Others think I was part of some free television and baby giveaway promotion. Whatever. All I know is that now I have certain mysterious audio-visual-techno superpowers, and that very TV is now part of my Amazing Techno Dude costume.

Here's the deal: I'm technically the Bodacious Backwards Woman's sidekick, but I should be her partner. I repeat: *I should be granny's partner by now! I should! I should! I should!*

Last week I brought this up while she was doing her backwards workout. How she manages those reverse toe-touches I'll never know. I guess she's just a very limber old backwards lady.

"Granny, I'm growing up. In fact, I think I'm old enough to—"

But Granny didn't let me finish. "Me catch to enough old!" she said, taking off running backwards down the street. She's kind of a backwards exercise nut.

I called after her even though she was long gone.

"Hey, Granny! I should be your partner! It's long overdue! Long overdue!! You still think of me as a kid, which I'm not! Obviously! Duh!"

When I was little, I was totally thrilled to tag along with her. I really loved it when she yelled her famous

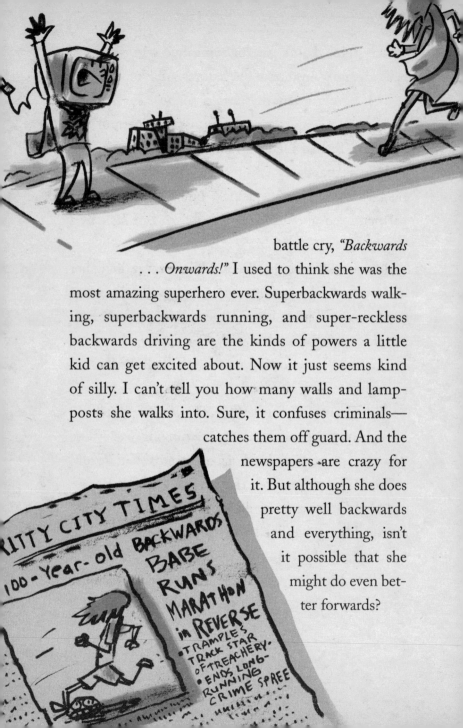

battle cry, *"Backwards*
. . . Onwards!" I used to think she was the
most amazing superhero ever. Superbackwards walking, superbackwards running, and super-reckless
backwards driving are the kinds of powers a little
kid can get excited about. Now it just seems kind
of silly. I can't tell you how many walls and lampposts she walks into. Sure, it confuses criminals—
catches them off guard. And the
newspapers are crazy for
it. But although she does
pretty well backwards
and everything, isn't
it possible that she
might do even better forwards?

ITTY CITY TIMES

100-Year-old BACKWARDS BABE RUNS MARATHON in REVERSE
• TRAMPLES TRACK STAR
• OF TREACHERY
• ENDS LONG-RUNNING CRIME SPREE

And then there's the whole super-backwards-talking thing: "Guys bad, out look!", "Come I here!", or "Pie sweetie techno amazing, much so-o-o you love I!" I mean, gimme a break. It's like growing up in a bilingual nuthouse.

Don't get me wrong, I love her and everything. She took me in, fed me, clothed me, and still bakes me her Super-Chew Choco-Chunk Crusty-Crunch cookies whenever I ask, even after midnight, even after I've brushed my teeth. Imagine the best cookie you've ever tasted, and multiply that by infinite infinities, and your cookie wouldn't taste one tenth as good as Granny's. And she's the only person in the world who can make me laugh until my face, stomach, and eyeballs hurt. She once un-ate an entire eleven-course meal at a fancy dinner at the mayor's house, using absolutely perfect table manners except for the fact that the food was coming out instead of going in. I almost died laughing. Mayor What's-His-Name was not amused.

Plus, over the years, Granny and I have brought many world-class supercreeps to justice, including Terrible Toejam Man, Superbad Boogermonkey, and, of course, Queen Smellina, the Shrieking Stinkbug of Stench.

And, oh yeah, the Bodacious Backwards Woman's other superpower is time travel. I didn't mention it at first because she doesn't do it much anymore. It was never the kind of thing where she would go way, way back, like to the Middle Ages or prehistoric times or something. Anyone who's ever read a book or seen a movie knows that that type of show-offy time travel only gets you into trouble anyway. Like, you accidentally bring something weird back with you that doesn't belong in your time, or you swat a million-year-old mosquito and the whole history of the world goes bonkers.

"That needs who?" the Bodacious Backwards Woman always says.

No, she would only go back a few hours or minutes, just to make some little changes. Like when she went back seventeen minutes to tiptoe into Gerald the

Super Jerk's lair and duct-tape the glass door of his shower closed. He was in there getting ready to go on a super-jerky crime spree, which of course he had already done in the present. But Granny fixed it so he never did those crimes. Because he could never get out of that shower. He's gotta be pretty pruney by now.

Recently, her going-back-in-time abilities have been—well, unreliable, to say the least. She'll try to go back an hour and instead maybe go forward three or four seconds. Blink and you miss it.

Meanwhile, not having the time-travel option is a pain. I've been working on a technique involving the Rewind and Fastforward buttons on my remote, but I haven't quite worked it out yet. It's harder than it looks. The closest I've come to time travel is giving myself a bad headache that lasts well into the future.

I'm always working on other new powers too, and believe me, they're way better than backwardsness. I'm into video and computers—all the newest stuff. The only problem is we can't afford all the newest stuff. Actually, we can't afford any of the newest stuff, so I have to build my own.

CHAPTER 4:
problem Bad/solution worse

By the way, there's nothing secret about our identities. We are who we are. Granny really is a super backwards person and I really am a super TV-headed person and everyone knows we lived alone in a large shabby house at 1313 Thirteenth Street for the longest time. Then, this Thursday, as you know, the chimney collapsed, the toilet exploded, and the doorbell caught fire.

"These are very expensive repairs and we are very broke!" I said, coughing and holding my nose.

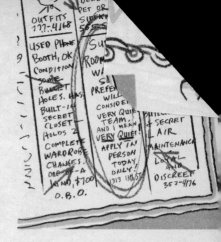

"Roommate a get will we!" Granny replied.

"Oh, please, Granny. Taking in a roommate is the worst idea ever," I said.

But we needed the money, and since we weren't partners, I didn't get a vote. Did I mention we should be partners?!

Anyway, we couldn't get a regular roommate because regular people can't possibly take the super-stress we live with every single minute. So we put an ad in the back of *The Super Globe Gazette*. At the crack of dawn the next morning there was a line of superdudes and -dudettes around the block. No super anybody that anybody's ever heard of, though. We're talkin' the kind who can't afford the fancy mansions, the fancy butlers, and the superfancy secret lairs.

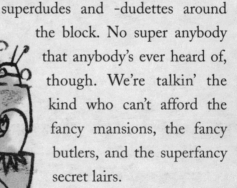

Speaking of which, our lair is in the kitchen. The

SUPER
SODA
SUPER
SOAP
SUPER
SOUP

secret gadgets and gizmos are hidden away in foldout, drop-down drawers and cupboards. It transforms from a tiny ordinary kitchen to a tiny high-tech lair in 2.8 seconds. It's got all the solar, infrared, digital, electromagnetic, videographic, mainframed frappinators and ding-a-ma-jobs I've figured out how to frazzerate.

Okay, that made no sense. I don't know the jargon. I just make cool stuff.

Basically, the lair is perfect for plotting superfiend-busting strategies. Plus the fridge is right there, chockful of supersnacks.

And now we would be sharing it all with a stranger.

CHAPTER 5:

Meet and Greet

At eight o'clock sharp, superfists started pounding on the front door—until they knocked it down. So that was one more thing we'd have to fix. Plus, the house shook so hard, about thirty medals and trophies fell off their mantels. That heavy new trophy landed right on my head, which made me hate it even more.

Superfreaks started filing in and we handed out applications. Granny was way too nice to them, running backwards to and from the kitchen to get them sodas and treats. Then Granny and I sat down at the dining room table.

"First who's?" said Granny.

"Blimey, old girl, you're lookin' at 'im!" said someone in a nasal British accent.

But there was no one there.

"Oh, please," I said, " not the Invisible Manatee. He would be impossible to live with—no way to know he's there until he sits on you, all nine hundred pounds of him."

"I'm down here, beanpole!"

We peered over the table edge to see an angry pair of jockey shorts, size extra small, shaking a fist at us.

"A pair of underpants?" I laughed. "What's so super about *you*?"

"One t'ain't got to be huge to be super, ye know. Me mum happens to be the Battlin' Bra of Birmingham and me dad is Jumpin' Jack Jockstrap—both superstars in the wild world of super undergarments!"

"Never heard of them," I said.

"Well, the one and only Terrifyin' Tubesock Lad is me second cousin!"

"Okay, okay, but who might *you* be?" I asked.

"I *might* be the Queen of England, but it's not bloomin' likely!" he snapped back. "I'm Mighty Tighty Whitey: Fantastic, Elastic, Sarcastic!"

"Well, you don't have to be so snotty about it," I said.

"Underpants is a lot of things, but snotty ain't one of 'em. If you want snotty, the Remarkable Runnin' Nostril's yer bloke. We worked flu season together once. I used me superstretchy powers to catapult 'im into a crazed crowd of superevil preschoolers. Worked like a charm. Once one of 'em little tykes caught the bug, they all caught it. Every last one of 'em was swept away by a rushin', gushin' tidal wave of—"

"That's enough!" I said. "First, I just ate breakfast.

Second, this interview is over. And third, I just ate breakfast."

Mighty Tighty Whitey glared at me. He quickly hammered a tack into the floor, slipped his waistband (really his headband) over the tack, backed up—stretching, stretching, stretching—and then let go with a high-pitched *thwannnnng*. He bounced off every surface in the room before landing with a *thwaaack* right in my face. He slid off, flipped over, landed on his feet in the middle of the table, and took a

bow. I was too disgusted to speak.

Granny wasn't. "Underpants talented very!" she squealed. "Away right in move!"

"What?!"

I couldn't believe she was letting this lunatic into our lives! We didn't even get to the part where we ask him how much he could pay in rent, whether he'd help with the cleaning, pitch in for groceries—the normal things you'd want to know. But before I could say anything, Granny shouted, "Next who's?!"

Next who's? She had already okayed one super-awful roommate and now she was looking for another?

"Excuse me, Granny. Granny?"

Up stepped super goon number two. His face was the color of pea soup and crisscrossed with stitches that were oozing something, possibly pea soup. He looked like the Frankenstein monster's uglier brother.

"HEAR ABOUT FIRE IN CIRCUS?!" he roared.

"Riddles love I!" said Granny.

"I give up," I said, and I didn't mean on the riddle.

"OKAY, I TELL YOU ABOUT FIRE IN CIR-CUS!"

But before he could, a spooky little bird girl with swirling eyes, wearing a jewel-encrusted turban, swooped down and landed on the monster's nose.

"It was in tents!" she chirped.

The others erupted in laughter as she flew a victory lap around the room.

The monster was not amused.

"ARRRRRGGGGHHHHH!" he wailed, shaking his huge green fists. "ALL MORNING TEENY BIRD WITH SPOOKY EYEBALLS RUIN JOKES! I FRANKENSTEIN PUNSTER! POUNDING BAD GUYS WITH SUPER-PUNNY ACTION IS PUNSTER'S MAIN SUPERPOWER! HOW YOU KNOW ALL PUNCHLINES, SMALL BAD BIRD LADY??!!"

"Because I'm Pooky the Paranormal Parakeet," she said, fluttering down to the table. "Seer of futures, reader of minds . . ."

"AND SPOILER OF JOKES!" cried the punster.

"Punster Mr., much so worry don't," said Granny, shaking Pooky's tiny wing in greeting. "Both you to welcome!"

"I knew you were gonna say that," said Pooky.

I rolled my eyes.

"I knew you were gonna roll your eyes," she said.

The Frankenstein Punster shook his fists and howled.

"I also knew he was gonna shake his fists and howl."

"He *always* shakes his fists and howls," I said.

We had now acquired the three worst roommates in roommate history, so I thought Granny might stop the interviews. No such luck.

"Please name your?"

"The Impossibly Tough Two-Headed Infant," snarled both mouths of both heads of the super-muscular two-headed baby wobbling toward us. I couldn't tell if the wobbling was because he/they were just learning to walk or if his/their diaper was full. I didn't have to wait long to find out.

"Diaper change, *now!*" they cried in harmony—one in a high voice (named Biff), the other very low (named Smiff).

"Unpacking start—adorable how!" said Granny. "Next who's!"

Someone hollered from outside the house: "No arms, no legs! No head, no shoulder! . . ."

And something crashed through the living room wall.

". . . one big chunk . . . *I'm Wonder Boulder!*" it said as it continued out through the opposite wall. We heard screeching brakes, screaming people, and crashing cars, and then Wonder Boulder returned, this time down through the roof, blowing holes straight through several floors before punching through the dining room ceiling and knocking the Frankenstein Punster out cold.

This Wonder Boulder guy was just a big old block of granite with a cape. Not even a nice cape. He was the perfect guy to say no to. I mean, a rock couldn't have a lot of feelings to hurt. Plus, he was well on his way to destroying the house, which would kind of defeat the purpose of having roommates.

But Granny found him to be a "citizen solid" and added him to the list.

Next up was a teenage girl. She was very cute until she opened her mouth.

"Okay, like . . . who's spoiled rotten and darn proud of it?"

"Who girl, who girl, who?" said everyone else.

"Who does no chores; she's high above it?"

"Who girl, who girl, who?"

"Who needs con- stant rides to and from the mall, unlim- ited closet space, and if at any point she is not the center of attention, she will, like, instantly employ Super

Pout, which triggers a two-minute warning 'til Super Tantrum?"

I was getting super irritated.

"Who, girl, who girl, who?"

"SuperSass CuteGirl . . . *that's* who!"

"Girl, home sassy your is home sassy my!" giggled Granny.

I was beside myself. "Please, Granny, give me a break."

"Yes, *zap-zowee-whamma-gramma* . . . the boy needs a break!" said a large, muscular guy in a red Spandex suit and Hawaiian shirt. Finally, a real superhero. He had a deep, booming voice and even made his own sound effects.

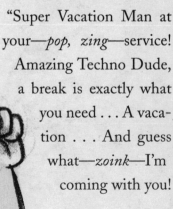

"Super Vacation Man at your—*pop, zing*—service! Amazing Techno Dude, a break is exactly what you need . . . A vacation . . . And guess what—*zoink*—I'm coming with you!

Kapow! Go-karts! Water skis! Drinks with little—*zip, bang, boom*—umbrellas! Super cotton candy 'til we—uh oh, look out . . . *splat!* Okay . . . so what are we waiting for? Let's go, go, go!"

"You must be joking," I said. "I've got school and all my super duties . . . plus we're totally broke. This is the worst possible time to go away."

Super Vacation Man's face fell. He made a sound like a deflating balloon and actually got smaller. A single tear trickled down his chiseled cheek.

"All my powers have to do with vacations: super surfboardin', super fishin', super lazin' by the pool," he sobbed, "and, sure, I use those powers on the job, but I never actually get to use them for—*zowee, zing,*

kablooey—fun! I'm *called* Super Vacation Man . . . but I've never *been* on a single *vacation*!" He spluttered like a motorboat running out of gas.

While I was wondering how "lazin' by the pool" could possibly be considered a superpower, Granny announced that "Man Vacation Super" was moving in and I should draw a warm bubble bath in my old kiddie pool and find him a glass of pineapple juice, so he could relax in vacationlike comfort until he calmed down. Or at least stopped blubbering.

Just then, something exploded in the basement, followed by that same something running up the stairs and crashing into the basement door. Then we heard it bounce back down the stairs, land with a thud, and howl in pain. Next, a very loud growl, up the stairs again, crash, bounce back down again, more howling. I opened the basement door, just in time to

see a small, caped dog on fire, billowing smoke, sprinting up the stairs, head down, tail up, snarling. He lunged at the now-open door and flew into the room, pieces of his teeth scattering across the floor.

I looked down at the smoldering dog. He was grinning stupidly, lying on his back with his legs straight up.

"I comed troo da furnace for show you jest how smartish and sneekishy I is," he said. "Now, somebudda, anybudda, please rub the bootiful belly of Blunder Mutt!"

While everyone coughed from smoke, Granny rubbed Blunder Mutt's belly. "Dog good!" she said.

"Dog kookoo!" I objected, but I knew Granny had already made up her mind.

He volunteered to be Official Super Phone Answerer and then tripped over the phone cord and fell back down the basement stairs.

"Perfect!" I called to him.

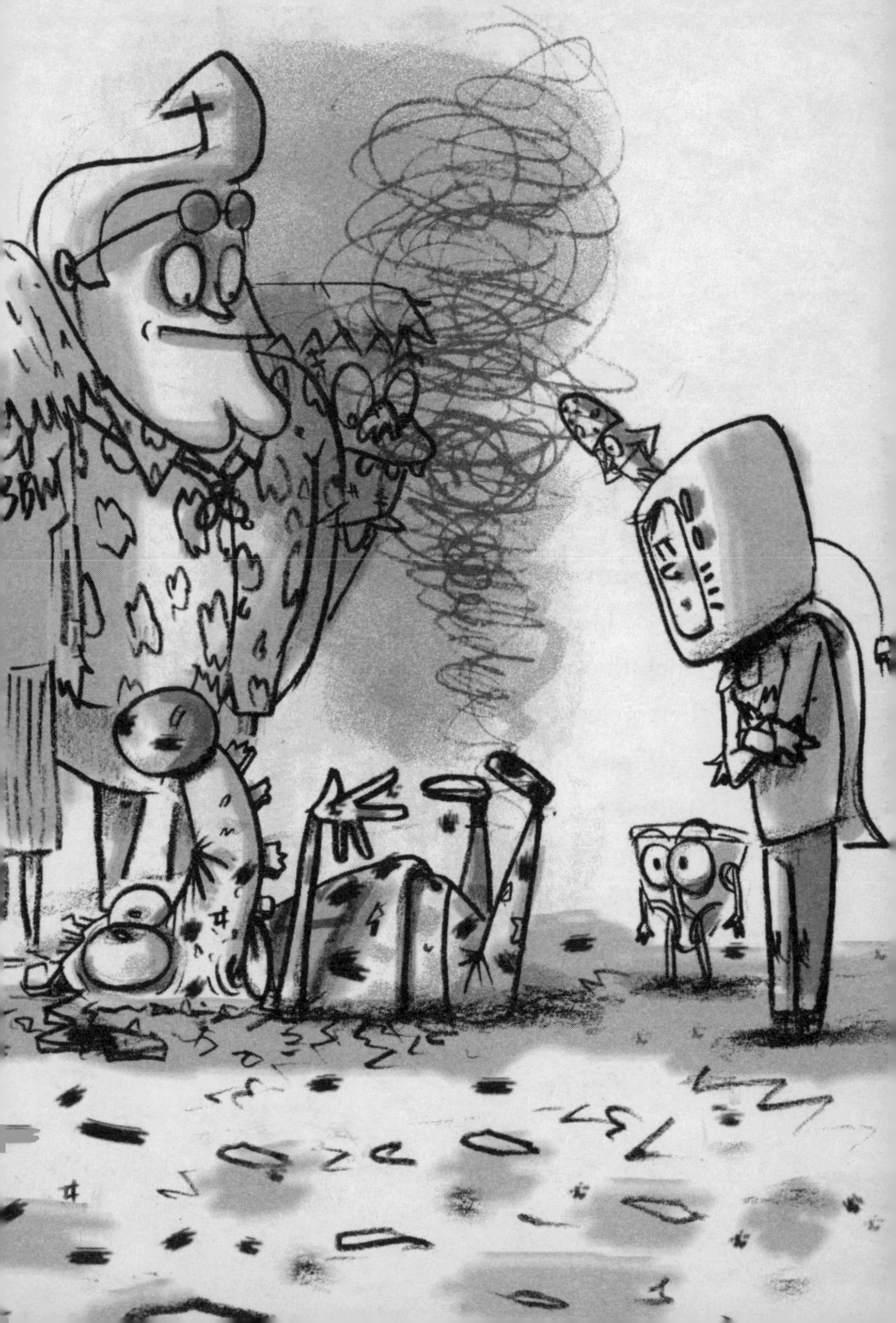
SBW

CHAPTER 6:
Fabian

Hard to believe, but it wasn't over. There was one more interview, which shall forever linger in my mind and nostrils.

The room went dark as a chubby young superkid shuffled in. He was glowing putrid yellow and gave off a smell that made everyone faint.

When we came to, he addressed us in a whining grunt.

"Greetings, Ms. Woman and Mr. Dude. Today will go down in super history as the day you were offered the once-in-a-lifetime

chance to live in close quarters with Fabian the Fabulous Flatulent Fellow. So . . . what do you say?"

"*Yes!*" said Granny.

"*No! No! No!*" I yelled.

I threatened to leave home if Granny didn't stop the madness right now.

So she did.

"Mr. Fellow," I said, "there is no room for you."

"Excuse me?" grunted Mr. Fellow.

"There is no *excuse* for you, either," I grunted back.

"Just for that," he replied, "I'm now Fabian the Fabulous Flatulent *Fiend*!"

and he crossed over to the dark side as easily as one crosses the street. Then he walked out the door and actually *did* cross the street, disappearing into a yucky yellow fog.

So that was that. We sent the other waiting super hopefuls away, too. In the end, we hadn't found one good roommate, we'd found eight—count 'em, eight—really *bad* ones. Nine, if you count the terrible two-headed tyke as two.

CHAPTER 7:
saturday

Moving-in day was a nightmare. Superheroes are super lazy when they're not on duty, and nothing brings it out like lugging heavy boxes up lots and lots of stairs.

The Impossibly Tough Two-Headed Infant, by far the strongest of the bunch, kept whining and complaining about superchild-labor laws.

"We demand regular bottle and poopy breaks!" they cried.

It was obvious that all these nuts had problems. And that together they would cause new, more complicated problems. The kitchen/lair was tiny. Our only bathroom was tinier. And there weren't nearly enough bedrooms.

"Okay, buddy up, 'cause everybody's gotta share a room!" I said.

"Okay, we'll share!" yelled Biff and Smiff. "Just the *two* of us, though. Believe me/us, two's already a crowd."

A high-pitched squeal pierced every super eardrum in the place. "Excuse me," said SuperSass CuteGirl, "I'll only share a room with my friends—like my shoes, my outfits, and my mint collection of superteen magazines. And, like, that's it! Because—who always gets her way through supersassiness and cuteness?"

Nobody was in the mood to ask, *Who girl, who girl, who?*

I could see we were getting nowhere. I'd have to match them up myself.

"SuperSass, you're with Pooky, because you're the only two girls."

"A filthy bird? I feel a Super Pout coming on."

"I knew you'd say that!" said Pooky.

"I knew you'd say you knew I'd say that!" screamed SuperSass.

"Enough!" I yelled. "Okay, Wonder Boulder: you go find a room with the Frankenstein Punster. Only a fellow of your density could stand those puns. Mighty Tighty Whitey, you've got the Impossibly Tough Two-Headed Infant."

So far, everyone was very unhappy with the sleeping arrangements. Ask me if I cared.

That left Super Vacation Man and Blunder Mutt.

"Super Vacation Man, here's a sleeping bag, so just pretend you're on vacation and camp on the couch. Blunder Mutt, you get to camp on the floor! What fun!"

This was probably the best matchup. SVM's eyes lit up when he saw the sleeping bag. And Blunder Mutt—well, he was just a superhappy guy.

But among the others, supersquabbles broke out all the time, and by nightfall, everyone was sick and tired of everyone else.

"Lunatics super of bunch a what!" sighed Granny, climbing the stairs backwards.

"Hello? I've been saying that for eight hours, except, you know, *forwards*!" I said, rolling my eyes. "Granny, I'm not too sure about this whole roommate idea. Actually, I am sure: very bad idea. More like a bad dream.

And I've been trying to tell you something: I think I'm old enough now to—"

But she interrupted me: "Are you spunky and cute how look!" She smiled.

Now this was insulting. "I'm not cute! I'm not spunky! I'm serious!"

"Cookies of batch a you baked I . . ." she said.

"Sorry, Granny, but cookies aren't going to cut it."

Okay, you already know how much I love her cookies. But I was fed up and didn't want to give her the chance to shut me up with comfort food.

"Sure you are?" asked Granny.

"Sure me are . . . I mean, yes I'm sure!"

"Night good and worry don't, then okay," she said, diving face-first under her covers and fluffing her pillow with her feet. "Backwards . . . onwards," she whispered as she drifted off.

"Right, backwards, onwards, worry don't," I said,

but I was plenty worried. I was having enough trouble living with Granny. Adding eight or nine insane roommates to the mix would give trouble a whole new meaning.

I went to bed, but it was hard to sleep with super goofballs bouncing off every wall in the house. Plus, I couldn't stop thinking about how the heck I was gonna break out of the whole sidekick thing.

If I couldn't get Granny to listen to me about becoming a partner, maybe I'd have to find somebody else. Maybe I needed a sidekick of my own. Somebody to boss around who'd make me look good. Perhaps one of our crazy roommates would do. Any of those lame-o's would make me look good.

The house was finally quiet, except for the Frankenstein Punster's snoring. The deep rumbling made everything vibrate, as if the whole house was snoring. I tiptoed downstairs for a glass of water. Super Vacation Man was sleeping standing up, clutching his suitcase. Under his other arm was the rolled-up sleeping bag. He was wearing sunglasses, a bathing suit, and flippers. He had sunblock slathered all over his face. Blunder Mutt was sprawled on his back on the floor with his legs straight up in the air again. He was drooling and mumbling softly in his sleep: "Please rub da belly . . . somebudda *please* rub da supa belly . . ."

Either of these two loons would definitely make me look good, but I also couldn't imagine having them along during an emergency. More likely they would *cause* an emergency.

I went back to bed, but still couldn't sleep, so I practiced my High-Def Video-Zombie Hypno-Stare. This was a new superskill I'd been working on. You know how watching TV turns you into a zombie? Well, I'd be able to do the same to supervillains merely by staring really, really, really hard into their eyes, while thinking about all the bad TV I'd seen in my life. It was a totally awesome super-power, but it didn't quite work yet. So far, I could only get a small hypno-ray going. It worked well on tiny, weaker supercreeps like Not So Rotten Ratman, Somewhat Slimy Salamander, and Barely Bad Barn Owl (The Unterrible Trio)—they're still walking around in a bad-sitcom daze. But I wouldn't dare try it on someone like Queen Smellina, the Shrieking Stinkbug of Stench, for instance. Her evil is so evil, using the High-Def Video-Zombie Hypno-Stare on her would be like trying to put out a forest fire with a squirt gun.

I finally conked out and had a weird dream. I was still me, but I was attached to Queen Smellina, sorta like Biff and Smiff. I was wearing jockey shorts on my head. Boulders were falling from the sky like huge hailstones. I kept saying,

"Listen, you cute and spunky sidekick, do as you're told!" But she did whatever the heck she wanted, which was mostly just blowing holes right through me with her bad-breath ray. Instead of blood, pea soup was gushing out of all the holes. My Hypno-Stare was useless against her, and I was drowning in a boiling, soupy sea, surrounded by spiral-eyed dog-sharks. My hypno-stare didn't work at all in the dream. But when I woke up, every fish in my aquarium was in a deep TV-zombie trance.

CHAPTER 8:

Scrambled Mayhem for Breakfast

Sunday, the day of rest. Yeah, right.

Morning broke to the sound of breaking glass and *very* loud burps. I ran down to the kitchen and discovered Wonder Boulder hurling himself around the room. He had already broken all our plates and now had the Impossibly Tough Two-Headed Infant cornered in the pantry.

"Those belching brats think that just because I don't have a nose they can burp in my face any time they want!" said Wonder Boulder, chasing Biff and Smiff into the dining room.

"News flash, pebble brain! You don't have a *face*, either!" screamed the double baby.

Meanwhile, at
the breakfast table,
the Frankenstein Punster
was still angry with Pooky about
her punchline-spoiling.

"SHUT BEAK, BIRD!" he grunted. "OKAY," he continued, addressing the others, "THIS GOOD ONE: HEAR ABOUT FIRE IN SHOE FACTORY?"

But again Pooky chirped in: "Not a sole survived!"

"ARRRRGGGGGGHHHH!" howled the frus-trated monster, clench-ing his fists so tightly that pea soup spurted around the room.

Super Vacation Man laughed like crazy. "Oh, Pooky, you are a trip!"

"A trip I don't wanna go on!" screamed SuperSass, emerging from the bathroom. "You try falling asleep with those creepy eyes spiraling and glowing in the dark all night!"

"At least she doesn't hog the bathroom all *day*, little miss hissy-fit!" said Mighty Tighty Whitey, stretching himself back and shooting her right between the eyes with a cinnamon roll.

"That's it!" she cried. "I'm skipping Super Pout

and moving right on to Super Tantrum!"

And then all heck broke loose. Everybody's breakfast was suddenly flying around the room. I had a terrible ringing in my ears, but soon I realized that at least part of the reason was the phone ringing.

I reached for my Amazing Techno Dude Handheld Remote. It wasn't in its holster. Why are remotes always disappearing? I found it in the fridge. How it got there, I'll never know. Anyway, I aimed and paused all the superheroes in midair. They were motionless, floating like snarling parade balloons, surrounded by frozen explosions of milk, cereal, and jelly doughnuts. All except Blunder Mutt, who I'd left unpaused.

"Blunder, who is the official phone answerer?" I asked.

Blunder Mutt's eyes popped open wide and he fell off his chair, chipping a tooth on the tabletop. He picked up the phone.

"Hello! Blunder Nut, fishy phone answerer speeching!"

He listened, screwed up his face, and slammed the phone back down.

"I knew it!" he said. "It was just that stupidish guy saying he's Mayor What's-His-Name with some big urgy emurgy thingy how you gotta scoot down to the City Hallway or somewheres, like rights away, like it's soooo importanty and all, and blah, blah, blah . . . end of the worlds . . . blah, blah, blah! I mean, what's him problem anyhoo?! He's obvioushly got the wrong numbers and he already calling fifty-ten times this morming!"

"I beg your pardon?" I said.

The other super-heroes all unpaused and fell to the floor in a shower of break-fast food.

CHAPTER 9:
on the case

I woke up Granny.

"Grandson wonderful morning good!" she said, backflipping to a handstand.

"Please, Granny," I said. "Cut the cheerful stuff. There's trouble. Right here in Gritty City."

She adjusted her Bodacious Backwards Woman Cape and I tuned my Amazing Techno Dude Deluxe TV Helmet, featuring 4-D satellite tracking and 3031 channels of premium cable. Nothing good on, of course.

"To the Backwardsmobile!" I shouted.

We ran and leaped into the bucket seats.

Granny slammed the pedal to the metal and we took off like a rocket in reverse. "Backwards . . . onwards!"

I couldn't wait 'til I got my driver's license. No matter how many times Granny drove 180 miles an hour backwards through midtown traffic, it never got any less terrifying. And the Backwardsmobile had seen better days. The too-large, too-loud, purple, green, orange, and black convertible was riddled with holes and covered with dents, scrapes, and graffiti. Plus it rattled and spewed thick black smoke. Very embarrassing.

We arrived at Gritty City City Hall in four and a half seconds.

"What took you so long?" said Mayor What's-His-Name.

"Never than late better!" said Granny.

"What?" said the mayor.

"Exactly," I said. "*What* seems to be the problem?"

"Does Fabian the Fabulous Flatulent Fiend ring a bell?" he asked.

"Our bell caught fire," I said, "so he just knocked."

"That fiend is one fart smellow," explained the mayor. "He swiped every

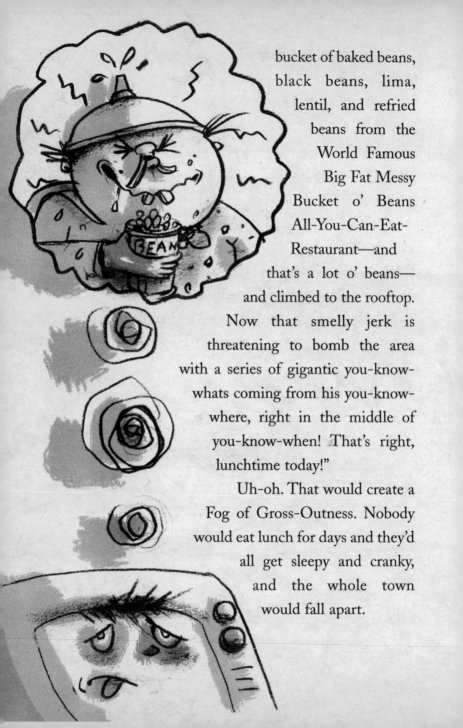

bucket of baked beans, black beans, lima, lentil, and refried beans from the World Famous Big Fat Messy Bucket o' Beans All-You-Can-Eat-Restaurant—and that's a lot o' beans— and climbed to the rooftop. Now that smelly jerk is threatening to bomb the area with a series of gigantic you-know-whats coming from his you-know-where, right in the middle of you-know-when! That's right, lunchtime today!"

Uh-oh. That would create a Fog of Gross-Outness. Nobody would eat lunch for days and they'd all get sleepy and cranky, and the whole town would fall apart.

"First, Gritty City," cried the mayor, "then North Gritty City, South, East, West Gritty City, and so on until every single city—including Gritty City's sister city, Itty Bitty City—will become Fabian's playground of yuckyness!"

"Why do these supervillains always feel the need to be so darn stinky and disgusting?" I asked.

"Disgusting and stinky always are things rotten!" said you-know-who.

"To the Backwardsmobile! Again!"

CHAPTER 10:
caught in a Brainstorm

The trip home took seven long seconds. Superbad traffic. I thought we'd never get there.

The other superheroes gathered in the living room.

"We need to think," I said. "And remember, there are no bad ideas in brainstorming."

"Okay . . ." said Blunder Mutt, raising an eyebrow, "how's about we just makes all the townpeoples wear clothespins on theirs noses for, ya know, ever!"

"Or, how about we all just go on *vacation*?! *Zip, kapow, shebang!*" shouted Super Vacation Man.

"Except *those* ideas," I said. "Those are bad ideas."

"Ideas terrible very, very," agreed Granny.

"Well, I think mine was super," said Super

Vacation Man, "because I've never had a vacation! Ever!"

"You know what, Super Goofballs? We don't have time for this. To the secret lair!" I cried, and we stepped into the kitchen.

CHAPTER 11:

chef Backwards the

I pressed the secret switch and the kitchen became the lair. All the superheroes oohed and aahed. I found the recipe I wanted and read it aloud as Granny and I went to work in our hyper tag-team style.

"Ready, set, concoct!

"One: Deep fry all secret ingredients separately in moldy lard for three hours over exceedingly high heat. I'm talking Earth's core hot.

"Two: Mix ingredients with wild/circular/swooping/punching/flailing motion." (A tiny tornado of fire erupted during the mixing process. But who really needs eyelashes anyway?)

"Three: Chop mixture using three to four flaming swords of different lengths.

"Four: Shove chopped mixture into bottle, using extreme force if necessary. Actually, even if not necessary. And, after a very long wind-up . . .

"Five: Toss bottle with perfect spiral, so hard you nearly dislocate your arm, into nearest cola-filled titanium triple-bonded trashcan.

"Six: Let sputter and boil until it's a blinding Day-Glo orange and blue, then remove, using two-ply radioactive-proof oven mitts. Make that seven-ply.

"Seven: Salt to taste.

"Eight: Voila! . . . Super-Sticky–Gas-Resistant–Anti-Stench Cement!"

The superheroes cheered!

Granny and I grabbed the jar of cement as well as a small suitcase holding a secret new invention we'd been saving for an emergency like this.

"To the Backwardsmobile again, again!" I shouted to Granny. "And then to the party store!"

The other superheroes cheered again, then stopped and looked really confused as Granny and I started to leave without them.

Except Blunder Mutt, who was still very excited. "Me loves party stores! Peas oh peas oh cheese oh peas? Can me go? Can me go?"

"Sorry," I said, "this is a job for real superheroes."

Blunder Mutt looked hurt. His tail drooped to the floor. But I'm sorry, if we took one, we'd have to take them all, and I wasn't about to cram all those super loonies into the Backwardsmobile. It's a two-seater.

The super-whining and -complaining started. We
ducked through a secret passageway and hopped into
the car.

Granny shouted, *"Backwards . . . onwards!"* and we
crashed into a police car parked directly behind us.

CHAPTER 12:
What's in Store

"Aren't you supposed to be in school, kid?" Sergeant Bub McButt frowned, standing beside the Backwardsmobile. He's always been jealous of our superness and acts like he doesn't know who we are.

Here's the thing. Okay, yes, I was supposed to be in school, but . . . well, I don't know, saving the world seemed a bit more important.

"*Sir*, we are on a mission for the mayor, *sir*!" I said, throwing in a snappy salute.

"Is that so? Do you have a license to drive that thing backwards, backwards stranger?" snarled McButt.

Granny was furious. "Woman Backwards Bodacious the I'm!" she said. "Brain kookoo silly you, world the save to way the on are we!"

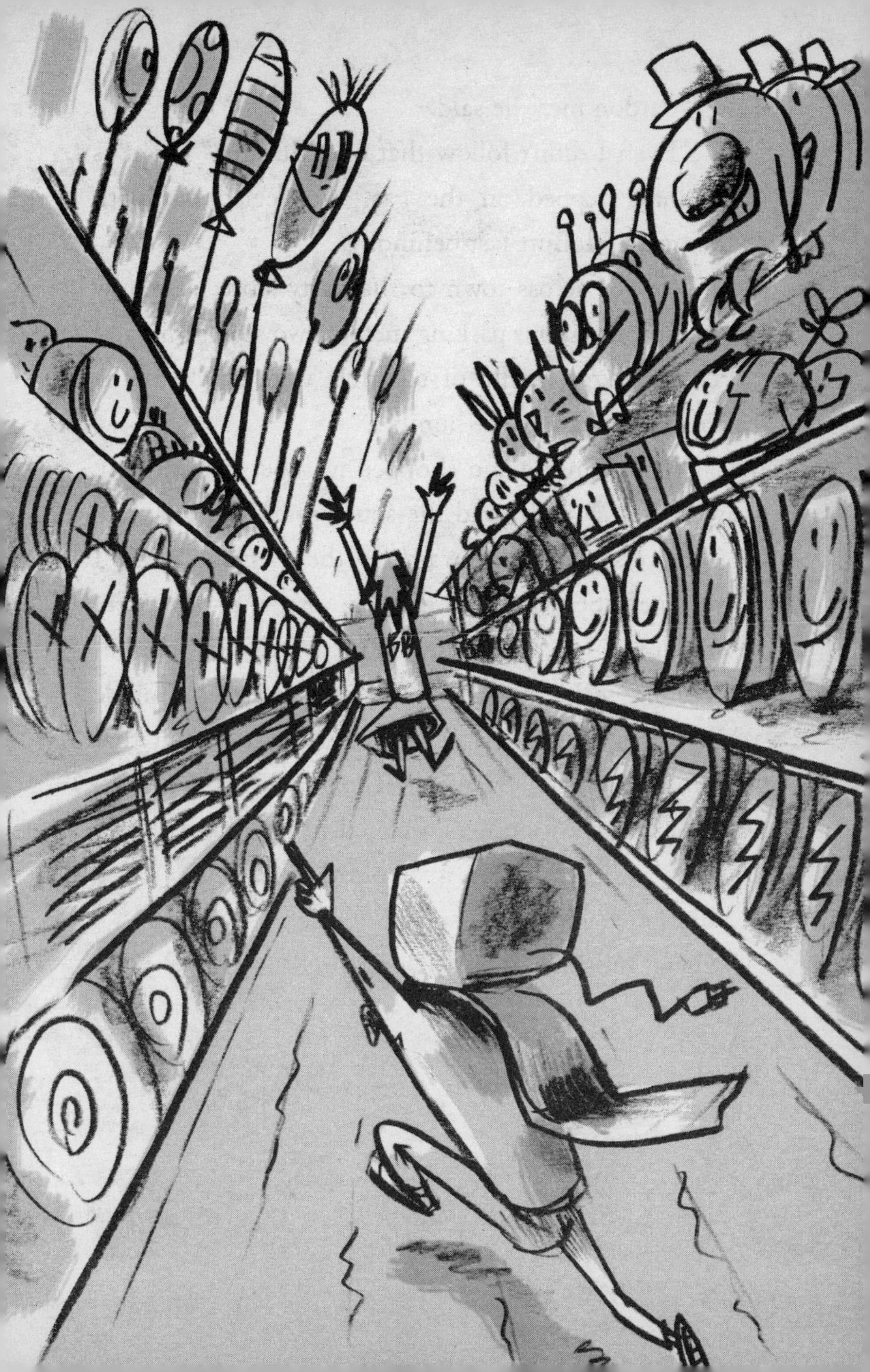

"Pardon me?" he said.

"Even I didn't follow that one, Bubster," I said as Granny stepped on the gas. We peeled out with Sergeant McButt fast behind.

We got across town to the party store in exactly two seconds. Four parking meters, two stop signs, and a very angry family of squirrels were stuck to the front—I mean, rear—bumper.

We ran inside and shopped in super-fast motion, with Bub McButt and the squirrels hot on our trail. Granny sprinted backwards to the checkout while I wrapped Sergeant McButt in crepe paper party streamers, like a mummy. I left a little air hole but couldn't resist sticking in a Long-Lasting Bubble Pipe. Sergeant McButt started to yell, but all that came out was an explosion of soap bubbles.

A group of toddlers, dressed in cute bumblebee-pirate party costumes, mistook McButt for some kind of fancy robotic piñata and chased him around

the store with plastic baseball bats. Their moms followed, screaming, "We want one! Where's the price tag on this thing!"

Granny paid, we hopped into the car, and sped off backwards, leaving Sergeant McButt, the toddlers, their moms, and the angry squirrels in the dust.

"Backwards . . . onwards!"

Granny started looking for potholes. Not just any old potholes: cosmic potholes. That's how she time travels. Some scientists think that time travel is possible by passing through wormholes or black holes, but Granny says, "Potholes cosmic beat can't you!" Who knows how she does it. I can't tell the cosmic kind from the regular. And, as I said, she's sorta lost the knack herself.

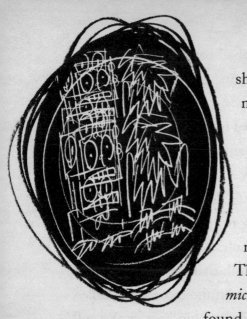

"*Pothole cosmic!*" she shouted. And *wham!*—my head bounced off the dashboard. Uncosmic for sure. It felt like we hit a truck. "*Pothole cosmic!*" she shouted again—and *kabammm! Totally* uncosmic. Felt like a *big* truck. Then, finally "*Pothole cosmic!*"—and *whooooosh!* She'd found one. We plunged into darkness and then through a blinding burst of wild lights and colors. We shook all over like we had our own private earthquake inside the car. Finally we screeched to a halt. We had reached the World Famous Big Fat Messy Bucket o' Beans All-You-Can-Eat Restaurant in negative seven seconds. It was normally a very short drive anyway.

"Thanks, Granny, but I don't think a few seconds are worth this gigantic bump on my head."

"*Know* just you, *think* don't you," she said, "work to travel time for."

"Whatever," I said, and fell out of the car.

CHAPTER 13:

Bean Crazy So Long!

Fabian the Fabulous Flatulent Fiend had eaten 99.999% of his hill o' beans. He was sitting on a hill o' empty bean buckets. He had gotten chubbier. Much chubbier. Like a balloon. And a lot crazier. Worse, he had one of those stupid karaoke microphones that he'd stolen from the restaurant.

His face was purple from ranting and raving into the microphone at the huge crowd gathered below. The people were screaming with fear, but Fabian thought they were his adoring fans adoring him.

"HELLOOOOO GRITTY CITY!" he shouted, and then started to sing. Who knew he was so multi-talented? The so-called melody was hard to follow, but the words went something like this:

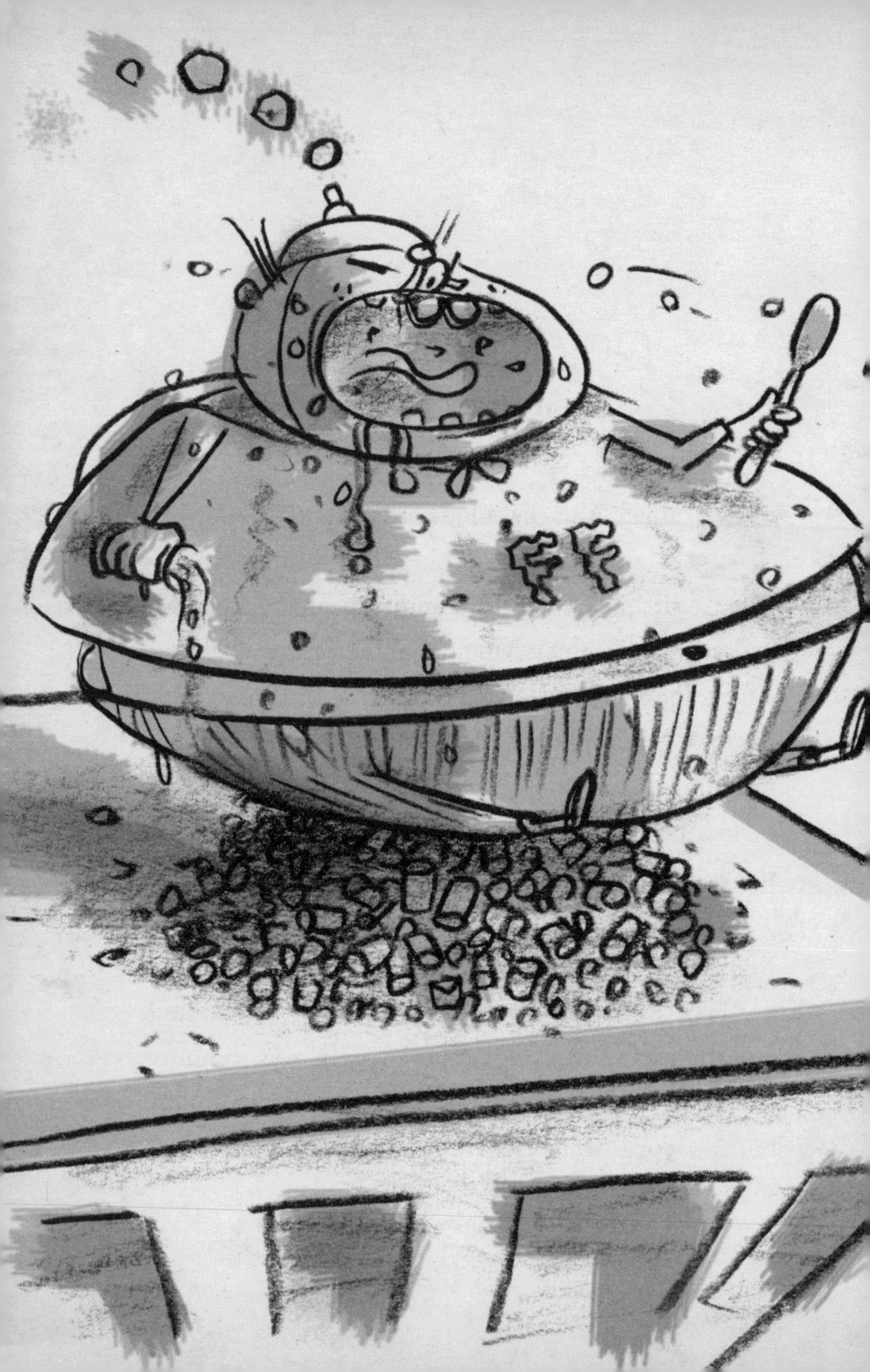

"I'M A BEAUTIFUL,
BEAUTIFUL BEAN,
THE GASSIEST BEAN
YOU HAVE SEEN,
YOU'D BETTER GET
READY TO RUN,
FOR SORRY YOU'LL
BE WHEN THE
LAST BEAN IS
DONE!"

"Oh, come on, Fabian! That makes absolutely no sense!" cried Mayor What's-His-Name, arriving in his car on the street below. "You claim to be a bean, yet you're *eating* beans! That, sir, is just plain wacko!"

"Well maybe wacko is what I've always *bean*!" He laughed back. "You get it? *Bean*?"

"That is *so* not funny!" shouted the mayor.

"Never debate what is and isn't funny with a diabolical nut job, sir," I said.

CHAPTER 14:

Fabian's Strong Suit

I checked my Amazing Techno Dude Deluxe TV Helmet. "Granny, the helicopter is three point two seconds away."

"Planned we as just!"

Then, activating my Amazing Techno Dude Stink-Vision Goggles, I got the expanding flatulent fiend in my sights. I ran some speedy calculations on his weight, mass, and waist and butt size. It was time to put our foolproof plan of *containment* and *disposal* into action.

Granny laid out our party store purchase:

BUTT SIZE: OFF THE CHART

eleven toddler-proof birthday party tablecloths, the
most durable material in the
history of the world. She
started cutting and gluing
so fast that I lost sight
of her in a flurry of fab-
ric. Granny has never
darned a sock in her
life—no time for

such things—but what she can do backwards with
a pair of safety scissors and a bottle of Super-
Sticky–Gas-Resistant–Anti-Stench Cement boggles
the mind. In no time she had produced the key
element of the *containment* phase: a very large, very
airtight diaper. Excellent.

We heard disgusting noises from above. Fabian
had finished the very last bucket o' beans.

"Oh, no!" I said. "Noxious gas is leaking out of
him, and not just from his you-know-where! It's coming out of his eyes, nose, and mouth, too!"

"Ewwwww!" went the crowd.

"Stinks really, really situation this!" shouted
Granny.

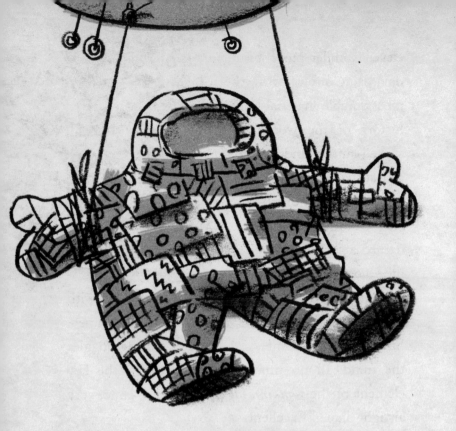

Boy, was she right. Things had gotten a lot worse, and our lower-body containment system would no longer be enough. We'd have to go full body.

"Problemo no!" said Granny, and with a few more *snip-snip*s and *glue-glue*s, we were ready.

The helicopter arrived and lifted Granny and me aloft with the Full-Body–Toddler–

Proof–Birthday–Party–Tablecloth–Patchwork Containment Suit. It looked like a very ugly space suit for a fat astronaut with extremely bad taste.

On the count of minus three, Granny shouted, "Time fitting it's!" and we put on our Antistink Masks and jumped to the roof.

As you might imagine, Fabian was even more disgusting up close. He flailed his arms and legs and fought us all the way. It was like trying to put a snowsuit on a gigantic, uncooperative, *really* stinky baby. And I thought the Impossibly Tough Two-Headed Infant was bad.

But somehow we finally got him into it: zipped, glued— *contained.*

Now for the *disposal* part of the equation.

"Drum roll, please!" I shouted, opening the tiny suitcase I'd been carrying around all day. All the workers and customers inside The World Famous Big Fat Messy Bucket o' Beans All-You-Can-Eat Restaurant helped out by drumming on Buckets o' Beans Collector Soda-Pop Cups.

"Yo! Your Flatulency! Behold the Amazing Techno Dude Stench-O-Matic Super Sucker! With one flip of this switch, you and your big, bad suit of barf-inducing nastiness will be sucked into oblivion . . . forever!"

The Stench-O-Matic is a tiny but

unbelievably powerful vacuum cleaner, specially designed for sucking up the smelliest of smell meisters. Truly the perfect gadget for disposing of stinking stankers like the Fabulous Flatulent Fiend.

"Granny, would you please do the honors?"

The Bodacious Backwards Woman cheered, "Nothing goes here!" and then "Backwards . . . onwards!" and flipped the switch. The contraption turned on with a loud *whoosh*!

I suppose I should have guessed that she would hold the Super Sucker backwards.

Granny was instantly sucked inside, headfirst, with a large, echoey *thoomp*! Actually, she got lodged halfway in, and the machine started spinning in circles, her legs kicking wildly on the outside.

"Noooooo!" I felt my face turn red as anger rose up in me. "I knew something like this would happen! This backwards stuff couldn't go on forever without something really bad happening!"

And then Granny called to me from inside the Sucker in an unbelievably cheerful voice. I mean, it was like she had no idea how serious this situation was!

"Sidekick, time next luck better, oops!" she said as she and the Super Sucker spun away.

"Sidekick?! That's it, I can't take it anymore! Listen carefully, Granny. I do *not* want to be your sidekick. I wanted to be your *partner*, but you wouldn't listen. So now I'll just be on my own. And I don't wanna hear another backwards word out of you! And don't come whining to me about being rescued, either. This is all your fault! Good-bye!"

Being stuck in the Super Sucker for a while would teach her a lesson. I would take care of Fabian on my own.

CHAPTER 15:

Going Solo

"**G**ood. Fantastic. I'm my own superhero. No more stupid sidekicking. I'll do things *my* way!"

I looked up at Fabian and noticed that his suit was beginning to inflate. It was only meant to be a short-term container, but now his ever-growing gassiness was causing the suit to grow larger and stinkier by the minute.

The suit got bigger ... and bigger ...

and bigger. I could hear Fabian's singing and other even grosser sounds rumbling and echoing from inside. Fabian and the suit started to float up into the air. I realized that if a gust of wind were to come along, he'd make an easy getaway without even trying. I couldn't let that happen, so I gathered some strips of leftover toddler-proof birthday party tablecloth and lashed him to the rooftop by his ankles.

"There. Problem solved. He's not going anywhere."

But since Granny was still inside the Super Sucker learning her lesson, I'd have to think of some other way of disposing of Fabian.

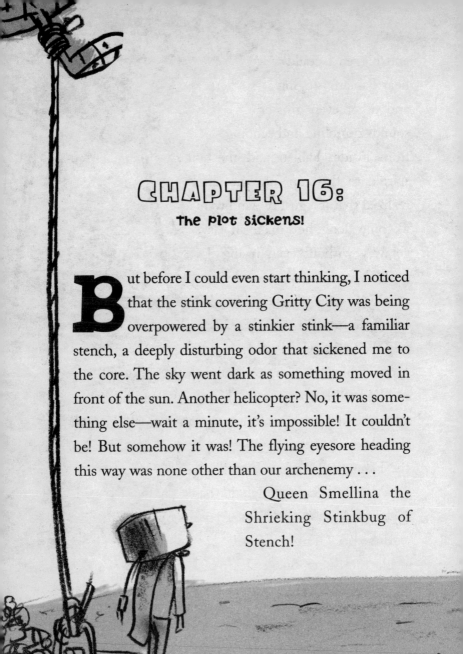

CHAPTER 16:

the plot sickens!

But before I could even start thinking, I noticed that the stink covering Gritty City was being overpowered by a stinkier stink—a familiar stench, a deeply disturbing odor that sickened me to the core. The sky went dark as something moved in front of the sun. Another helicopter? No, it was something else—wait a minute, it's impossible! It couldn't be! But somehow it was! The flying eyesore heading this way was none other than our archenemy . . .

Queen Smellina the Shrieking Stinkbug of Stench!

"YOO-HOO! SHORT TIME, NO SEE!" she cackled. "DID YOU MISS ME, TV-HEAD!"

"Wait a second," I cried, "how did you get out of jail? How on earth do you people always get out of jail?!"

"Front door," she said. "Turns out they did throw away the key, but they forgot to actually lock the lock first. I see you've met my new young sidekick, Fabian the Fabulous Flatulent Fiend!"

"Your sidekick? I should have known," I said. "The smelliness, the disgustingness, the stark-raving craziness!"

"I know, isn't he adorable?" she said, gazing up at the bloated monster. "I should really thank you," she continued. "Since you kicked him out of your stupid house, he hates you and ol' lady backwards even more than I do. Plus, he's so darn ugly, he makes me look good."

"You are one evil insect lady," I said. "And so very stinky."

"I STINK YOU MIGHT BE RIGHT!" she said. "*STINK*, INSTEAD OF *THINK*?" She laughed crazily for a long time. "HEE, HEE, HEE, HEE, HEE, HEE, HEE, HEE, HEE, HEE, HEE, HEE, HEE, HEE, HEE, HEE . . . !"

"So," I asked, "this whole flatulent fiend bean scheme is just part of a larger plot of *yours*?"

"Awww, look at you using your little brainy-wainy!" she said. "Try to follow me now. Yes, I'll take over Gritty City, and Itty Bitty City, and yes, I'll trash them all to make room for my beautifully smellicious

Kingdom of
Stench. But *way*
more delightful—listen up,
because this is quite an
honor—you and your granny
have been chosen to be my own per-
sonal slaves. And not just regular old
slaves. Goodness, no! You'll be the special
slaves whose job it is to keep my lovely stench
going. The Slave Stokers of Stench! Farming the
stench fields, toiling in the stench factory, stirring
the stench pots, taste-testing the essential stench
juices, and giving me hot, steamy stench baths and
long stench-oil massages. . . . I won't go into every
single yummy detail, but believe me, this job is quite
stenchy. I'm getting sweet, stinky goose bumps of
revenge just thinking about it."

"I'm getting sick just thinking about it." I said.

Meanwhile, the containment suit had gotten a lot
bigger. I mean, a *whole* lot bigger. It was now officially
a stinkier-than-air balloon.

The queen looked up at Fabian and chuckled. "I'm
getting a big sidekick out of this! Get it?"

"OH, MY WORD, QUEEN SMELLINA,"

Fabian called down. "BIG *SIDE*KICK ... INSTEAD OF BIG *KICK* ... NOW *THAT* IS A GOOD ONE! HA, HA ... VERY FUNNY, VERY CLEVER!"

"I KNOW, I REALLY CRACK ME UP! HEE, HEE, HEE, HEE, HEE!"

And then I heard a horrible sound and realized that down at street level, concrete was buckling, bricks were crumbling, and water pipes were bursting as the World Famous Bucket o' Beans All-You-Can-Eat Restaurant began to lift off the ground.

Smellina laughed louder and louder and crazier and crazier until she started to shriek.

SHRIEK! SHRIEK! SHRIEK!!!

"SHRIEK! SHRIEK! SHRIEK! SHRIEK! SHRIEK! SHRIEK! SHRIEK!"

Which was not a good sign. It was the same shriek Queen Smellina always makes when she's warming up for her dreaded Hyper-Bad-Breath Ray.

Then I heard Granny's muffled voice: "Here over, yoohoo!"

Man, oh, man! Granny had been in that Super Sucker for a really long time. I had to get her out, but Smellina was about to strike!

"SHRIEK! SHRIEK! SHRIEK! SHRIEK! SHRIEK! SHRIEK! SHRIEK!"

If only I'd brought the Bugzoid X-9000 with me! It had worked so well on Queen Smellina before; I knew it would work again.

Wait a minute—the roommates! They could take  the trusty Bugzoid out of storage and bring it to me. Hallelujah! I quickly dialed my Amazing Techno Dude Deluxe TV Helmet and called home. Man, oh, man! I . . . love . . . roommates!

CHAPTER 17:

Barking up the wrong mutt

Since Blunder Mutt should be answering, I sensed that eye contact might be important. Luckily, I had recently installed a small video screen in the handset of the home phone. I pressed Video Call and my screen flashed on.

"Okay, ringing . . . ringing . . . c'mon ol' Blunder, pick up, pick up . . . for the love of all that is super and heroic . . . please pick up!"

The screen flickered . . .

"Hello?! Blunder Gutt! Fishy foner ants peeking!" he said, emerging from the static. He had a stunned

look on his face. He
was rubbing his chin and
removing pieces of
teeth from
his mouth.

"Blunder Mutt!
Hi! It's me, Amazing
Techno Dude!"

"Oh, *you*. You
who no takey me to
store of party!"

"Right. Sorry about that.
Really, really sorry. A million
apologies. But listen up—this
is *important*. May I speak to one of the *other*
roommates, please? Any of the others will do."

"You are out of luckishness! They goed to party
story to find you. And they not letting me come
either! You and they think you and they so smart, but
you and they so stupid because I and me the bestest
and the bunchest!"

"Oh, well . . . yes, that's right, Blunder, my boy. You
are the bestest. In fact, that's why I'm calling. I'm giving you a very important assignment."

"Importantish asininement?"

"Exactly—importantish asininement."

"I be Amazling Tekko Duder's sidekicker?"

I thought for a minute and took a deep breath.

The next words were difficult to say.

"Yes . . . you'll be Tekko Duder's sidekicker," I said.

"You promisey? Say you promisey."

"I promisey."

"I promisey too! Yes! Yes! Yes!"

"Okay, good . . ."

"Yes! Yes!"

". . . now, *listen!*"

"Yes, yes, yessy, yes!"

"Blunder! Stop yessing and listen!"

"Yes, be listing!"

"Okay, Blunder . . . run to the basement!"

"Be running!" screamed Blunder, and he took off, still staring at the phone's screen. As expected, he fell down the base-ment stairs.

"Okay, Blunder, get up, boy!"

He got up and spit out a few teeth. "Okay, now go to the storage room, second door on the right. Good . . . and open the padlock . . . Right five, left nineteen, right eighty-six . . . Be sure to go past the second number and around again . . . Yes, you got it! Now up on the top shelf, behind the Super-Demented Squid Vaporizer . . . you'll see the Bugzoid X-9000. It's a heavy, yet delicate, masterpiece of technology, so bend your knees and lift . . . and be careful not to drop it!"

"Yes! I a good sidekicker, duder dude! Yessy, yes?!"

"Yes, very good sidekicker. Okay, now catch the number thirty-seven bus and transfer to the number one forty-nine express and bring the X-9000 to the World Famous Big Fat Messy Bucket o' Beans All-You-Can-Eat Restaurant immediately. Even sooner! Got that? . . .

Blunder Mutt? . . . *Hello?!*"

After a long pause, Blunder Mutt spoke in a very spacey voice: "Ooohhhh . . . purty lighties on the X-Niner Thingy . . . so many lighties . . . so many buttonies . . ."

"That's right, Blunder, but don't touch any buttonies! Just run to the bus! *Bus* . . . not buttonies!"

"But soooo . . . sparklyish . . . sooooooo fancyish . . . I likey *red* . . . it sooo prettiest . . . I wanna touchy red button . . ."

"No, no, no! Listen, Blunder, repeat after me . . ."

"Reepy tafter me . . ."

"Do not . . ."

"Do snot . . ."

"Under any circumstances . . ."

"Blunder when he burp he dances . . . Hey, that's me!"

". . . touch the red button!"

"Touchy red button?"

"Touchy red button."

"Okay . . . Touchy red button!"

"No! *Not! Not* touchy red button!"

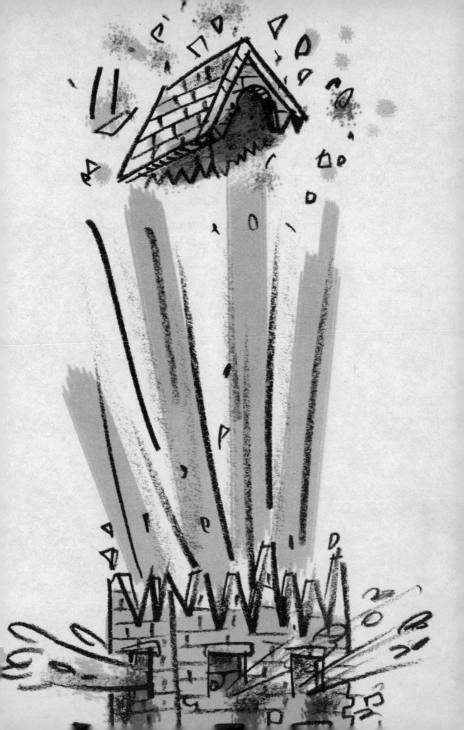

But it was too late. I watched as Blunder reached for the red self-destruct button, which I'd added in case the X-9000 fell into the wrong hands. I hadn't counted on the wrong paws.

He smiled a big, goofy smile. "Me, side kicker of Amazley Tekmoe Duker . . . Touchy red button . . . now!" and the screen went black.

"I . . . hate . . . roommates!" I shouted to the heavens.

CHAPTER 18:

I Think You Stink

Meanwhile, all of Gritty City was now covered in a thick brown mist.

Queen Smellina was still shrieking: "SHRIEK! SHRIEK! SHRIEK!"

Then she stopped.

Uh-oh, this was it: the calm before the bad-breath storm.

Queen Smellina smiled her evil smile, reared back like a cobra, and sucked in a deep breath. This time my shirt, cape, and all of the hair on my arms were ripped right off of me. She paused, then screeched one huge shriek, letting loose the biggest Hyper-Bad Breath Ray ever. It was a putrid,

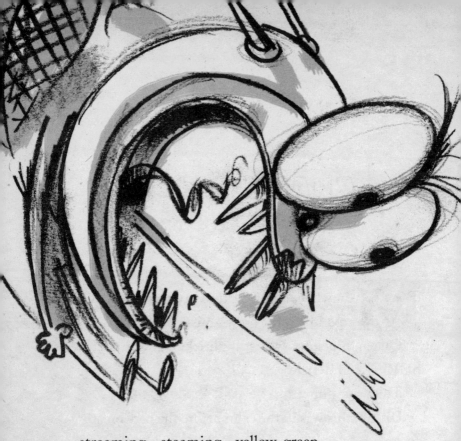

streaming, steaming, yellow-green
crackling and very icky laser beam, hot with toxic
stinkiness. . . .

And it was headed straight for me.

I needed a plan!

Wait! I could pause everything with my Amazing
Techno Dude Handheld Remote!

I reached for it. Oh no! It wasn't in the holster! It

wasn't anywhere! What *is* it with remotes?!"

Okay. What about my patented High-Definition Video-Zombie Hypno-Stare?

But it didn't really work that well yet!

But, but, but . . . This was no time for buts. I couldn't let Gritty City become the Kingdom of Stench. And I wasn't about to spend my life giving stench-oil massages to a disgusting insect lady!

So, I took a deep breath and also reared back like a cobra, paused, counted to three, and yelled, "Hypno-Stare *ON*!" Then I stared really, really, really, really hard—way harder than I had ever stared—into the evil eyes of Queen Smellina. My eyeballs nearly popped out of my head. I thought about every bad TV show I'd ever seen: bad sitcoms, bad game shows, bad shows made for kids that kids hate . . . And to my amazement, a gigantic, blue, glowing ray leaped from my eyes and shot straight toward Queen Smellina! It collided with her Hyper-Bad Breath Ray and both rays stopped right there, halfway between us in midair. They were of exactly the same strength.

I couldn't zombify her and she couldn't stenchify me!

I stared and she shrieked and blue video sparks and smelly green laser sparks shot like fireworks in all directions. We were deadlocked in a stalemate of superness!

Meanwhile, Fabian's fabulous flatulent balloon had become Fabian's fabulous flatulent blimp.

And that . . . was when . . . I saw . . . the spaceship.

Through the blue glow of the Hypno-Stare, I saw a spaceship descending through the clouds of stench, behind and out of view of Queen Smellina.

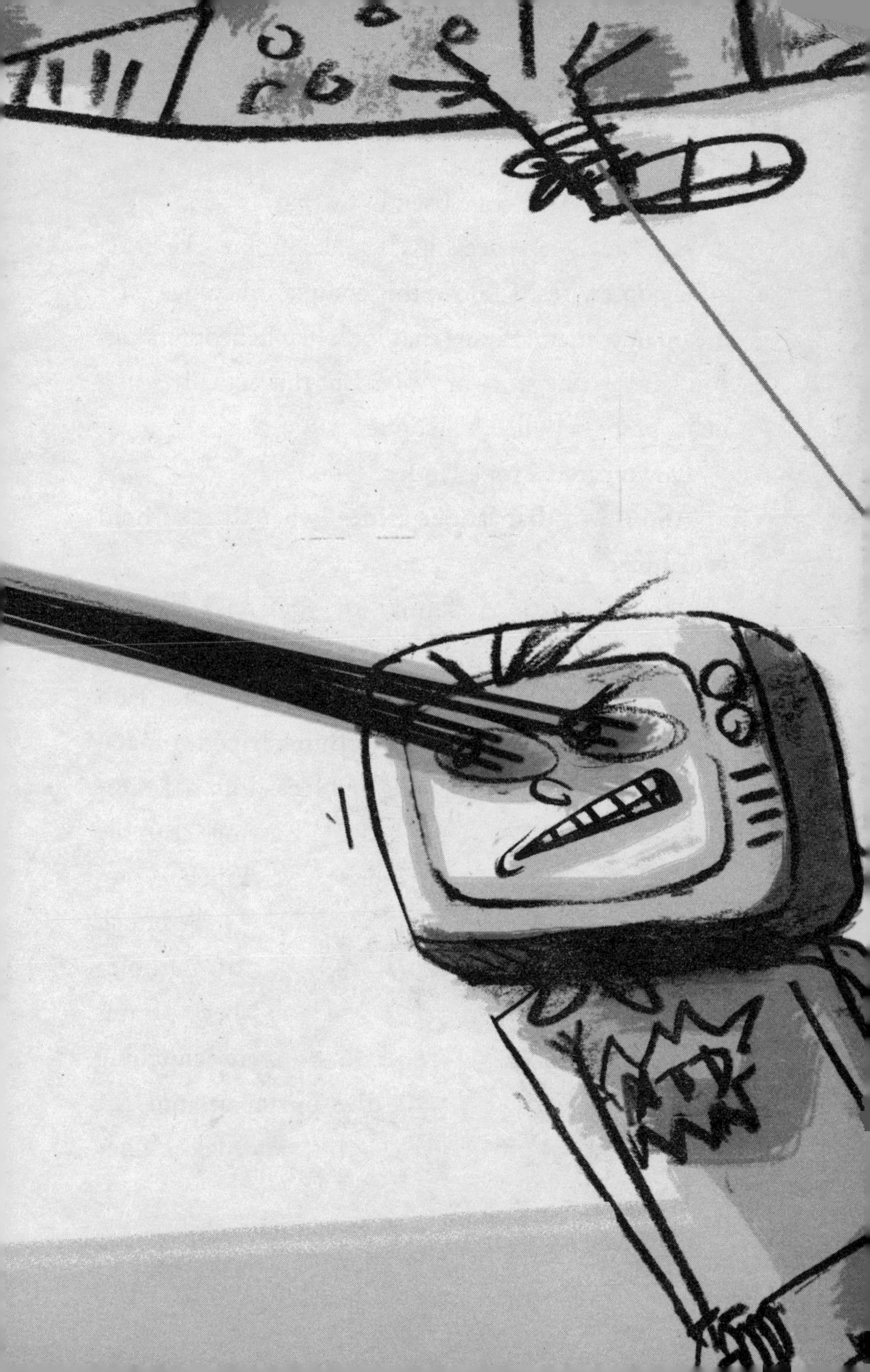

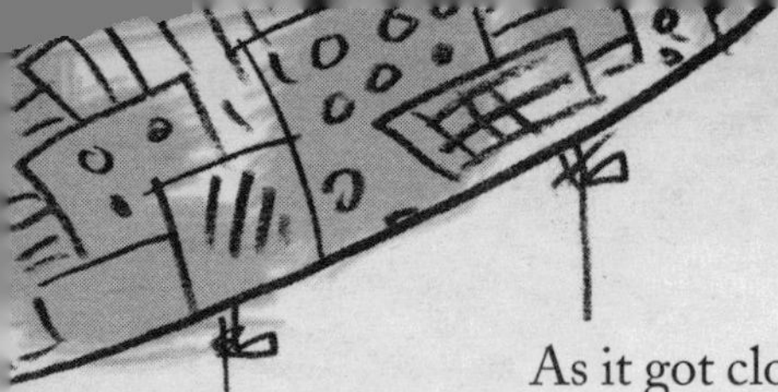

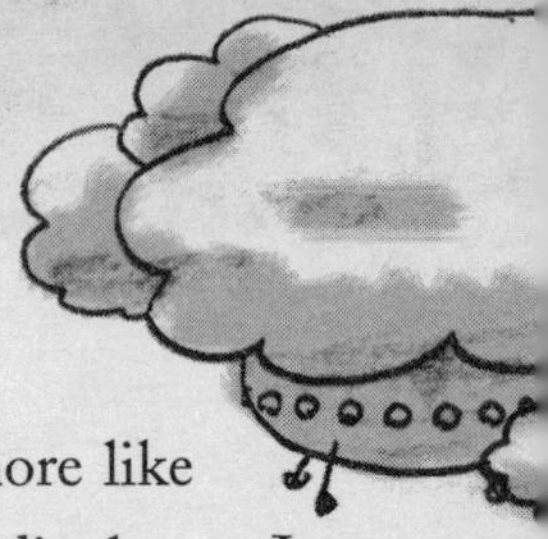

As it got closer, I saw that it wasn't really a spaceship. It looked more like a helicopter. Yes, I know, this sounds ridiculous—I mean, how many things that look like helicopters can you have in one story anyway? But this actually *was* a helicopter—a police helicopter!

Down came a rope ladder.

And down that ladder came—what the . . . hold your horses . . .

A family of squirrels, looking angrier than ever. And . . .

A Sergeant Bub McButt–shaped piñata, spewing bubbles from a Long-Lasting Bubble Pipe!

A bunch of bumble-bee pirates were clutching the piñata around the neck, arms, and legs. They

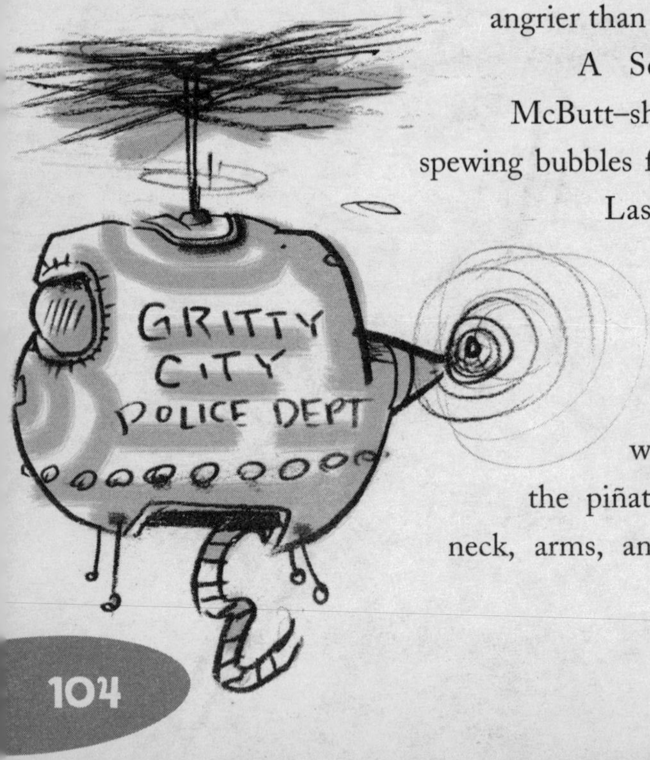
GRITTY
CITY
POLICE DEPT

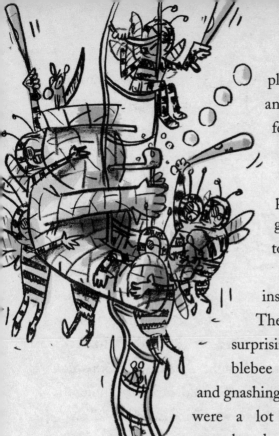

were swinging plastic baseball bats and kicking their feet wildly in the air. It was a curious sight. The piñata, the wriggling legs . . . all together it looked a little like a huge insect.

The toddlers made surprisingly scary bumblebee pirates, buzzing and gnashing their teeth. They were a lot bigger than I remembered. And there were *more* than I remembered: seven in all. Eight if you counted the two-headed guy as two. Two-headed guy? Wait a minute. Who were behind those fake beards and eye patches?

Yes, all the superheroes (except Blunder Mutt) had found Sergeant McButt and borrowed the toddlers'

costumes. I'm surprised to say I was happy to see those loonies.

I had a plan and I needed to talk to them without Queen Smellina hearing us. Maybe I could *think* a message to Pooky and she could pass it on to the others.

I tried to think loudly.

Buzz, buzz . . . ahoy! I thought.

Pooky smiled and thought, *I knew you'd think that.*

I was surprised that I could hear *her* thoughts. Apparently she had two-way mind-reading skills.

I continued to think at Pooky. *Ahoy and listen! The Bodacious Backwards Woman is stuck inside that sucker over there—the thing that's spinning like mad with the legs flopping around—and, well, I'm sorta in a battle of life and death here, and I really gotta keep this Hypno-Stare going or we're all, you know, doomed. So your job is to get Granny out of that thing now! Everyone except SuperSass, the Impossibly Tough Two-Headed Infant, and you, Pooky. You three keep buzzing and wiggling and looking like a huge hunky male insect. Got it? Or did you know I'd think all that, too?"*

Pooky winked and nodded.

So, why the heck did I waste all that time thinking all that stuff?

She quickly told the others.

SuperSass did a super-fast bugifying makeover of the piñata and then she, Pooky, and the two-headed Infant went back to buzzing and wiggling.

"Super sucker! Super buzz! Super arrrrrrgh!" whispered the rest of the roommates as the other three raced to rescue Granny.

CHAPTER 19:

Playing Cupid

"Yoo-hoo, Queen Smellina!" I called.

It was hard for her to answer since she was using her mouth to hack her ray at me:

"UTT OW ID?!"

"Oh, I don't know, I thought maybe you'd be interested to hear that Hunky Valentine, your one and only true love, is right behind you."

Her eyes glazed over. The Hyper-Bad Breath Ray stopped.

Just in time. My Hypno-Stare

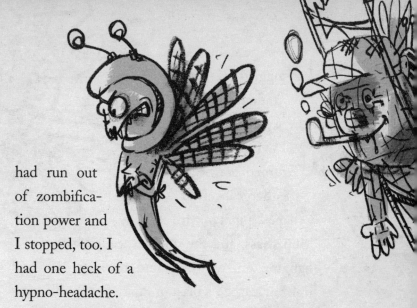

had run out
of zombifica-
tion power and
I stopped, too. I
had one heck of a
hypno-headache.

"HUNKY VALENTINE?" She sneered.
"YOU CAN'T FOOL ME! HUNKY-WUNKY
WAS A WOBOT. I MEAN, *ROBOT*. A HUNKY
ROBOT WITH DREAMY EYES, BUT *STILL!*"

"Ahh, Your Stinkiness, but I'm talking about the
real Hunky Valentine, the one I based that dumb
robot on. And he sooooo wants to meet you."

Her eyeballs bulged and turned heart-shaped. "Tee-
hee! I know you're pulling my hairy leg!" she said,
blushing. "Probably all six of them! Tee, hee, hee!"

"Why, Queenie, you are quite the catch for a cute
single insect guy. And I must say, I have never seen a
cuter one! I mean, if you're into that kind of thing."

She squinted and giggled. "I suppose it couldn't hurt to take a *teeny* peeky-poo . . ." Queen Smellina turned her head and saw the Sergeant Bub McButt–shaped piñata, with Pooky, SuperSass, and the double-headed baby hanging on, wiggling, and buzzing. Biff and Smiff unleashed a blast of rapid-fire double baby burps at the queen's face.

Direct hit! And boy, did she love that smell! "Oh, my dearest Hunky-Wunk," cooed Queen Smellina, "you are just *too* hunkerrific! It's not fair . . . I can't resist . . . I'm just a helpless little stinky stinkbug!"

The queen floated toward what she thought was her Hunky-Wunky, high above the World Famous Big Fat Messy Bucket o' Beans All-You-Can-Eat Restaurant, high above the street.

She shut her eyes and puckered her lips, inching closer and closer.

CHAPTER 20:

LOOK OUT

"**P**lant those delicious liver lips on me, you six-legged loverbug!" she squealed.

As the queen leaned in, Pooky, SuperSass, and the twins prepared to whack her with their plastic baseball bats. My plan was working perfectly.

But just then—guess who— Blunder Mutt fell out of the clouds and crashed onto the restaurant's rooftop. He'd been blown high into the sky when the Bugzoid

X-9000 exploded. It had taken all this time to come down. His fur was mostly burned off, but he had a huge smile on his face.

"Yo, Amazy Dude of Techno!"

The queen spun around. Pooky, SuperSass, and the Two-Headed Infant tried to whack her, but they whacked each other instead. The plastic baseball bats bounced off their heads and fell to the street below.

Queen Smellina didn't even notice. All she knew was that she hadn't gotten her supersmooch. And boy, was she angry!

She glared at Blunder Mutt.

She opened her mouth and arched her back.

You know what was coming.

Suddenly Blunder Mutt took off like a shot, leaping toward her. What the heck was he doing?

The queen released her Hyper-Bad Breath Ray, and Blunder took a direct hit. But it didn't stop him!

He bravely battled his way through it, like he was swimming against the current of a mighty, stinking river, then he flipped and landed inside the queen's mouth, feetfirst, plugging it up and stopping the deadly ray.

Everything stopped. Blunder Mutt's head was sticking out of the queen's mouth. He looked like a gopher peering from his hole.
He smiled a dopey smile and sickly green smoke drifted from his nostrils.

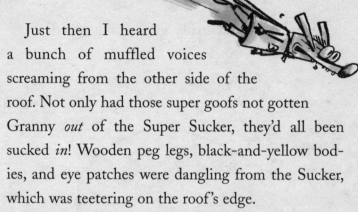

Just then I heard
a bunch of muffled voices
screaming from the other side of the
roof. Not only had those super goofs not gotten
Granny *out* of the Super Sucker, they'd all been
sucked *in*! Wooden peg legs, black-and-yellow bodies, and eye patches were dangling from the Sucker,
which was teetering on the roof's edge.

Queen Smellina looked at the contraption and
smiled. She took aim and spit Blunder Mutt out like
a stale piece of gum. He shot through the air and
slammed full force into the Sucker. I watched in horror as Mutt, Sucker, Granny, and everyone else tumbled over the edge of the
roof.

No! I reached for my remote, and of course it wasn't there. I watched them fall. I couldn't do a thing about it. I heard the tiny crash way down below.

Queen Smellina just laughed and laughed.

CHAPTER 21:

WOE IS ME

Granny, Blunder, and all the other bonkers-but-brave roommates—lost in action. *And it was my fault!*

I felt sick—as if life had kicked me in the stomach.

There was something else I felt. One not so amazing thing about being the Amazing Techno Dude is that sometimes, when I'm in trouble, my mind gets a bit mixed up, kinda like bad reception on a TV. It's like my wiring shorts out or my signal goes bad. My brain, my whole body, gets lost in a digital snowstorm of blips and bleeps.

I looked down at my hands and they were dissolving into flickering grains of color. My head felt exactly like my hands looked.

My brain was fried. Deep-fried. I couldn't think.

What would Granny do? And how would she do it?

I remembered something she'd said earlier. Something I'd barely even heard at the time. Something I could hear her voice repeating now.

Know just you, think don't you, she'd said, *work to travel time for.*

What was that? *Four* times *two* travel who . . . umm . . . wha—?

That couldn't be right. I felt like I'd turned into Blunder Mutt.

Take it slow.
For time
travel . . .
  . . . to work . . .
  . . . don't *think* . . .
  . . . just *know*?
Stop think-
ing and start
knowing?
Sounded crazy.

But then, without thinking, I reached for the remote. I somehow knew it would be there and it was. Right in my holster. Have you ever noticed that remotes magically reappear when you stop thinking about them?

It was way too late for Pause. I had to Rewind.

And now I knew I could do it.

I pointed the remote down at the street below, toward the cloud of smoke where the Super Sucker had crashed.

"Okay . . . *rewind*!"

What? No lights? No power? No nothing?

You have *got* to be kidding!

Have you ever noticed that remotes always stop

working for no rea-
son? Even when you
know you put new bat-
teries in them? I opened it
and wiggled the batteries
around—but still nothing.

So I did what everyone
does with a broken remote.

I slammed it against the
side of my helmet three
times—*hard*. Arrgh! Arrgh! Arrgh! Then I
slammed it six more times. Then I
shook it and punched it and pounded
it. Then I chewed on it.

Then I threw it on the ground
and stomped on it—just to make sure!

And then I picked up what was left
of it, and held the tiny pieces together in
my hands, and aimed it over the edge. I
pressed the button so hard my thumb
hurt. A lot.

"C'mon, c'mon . . . *Rewind*! Yessss!"

You'd be surprised what a little pounding and stomping can do.

I could see the Super Sucker flying back up toward me through the smoke. It was flying backwards in time. And so was I.

I was surrounded by a strange glow. I could see time rushing past. I saw Blunder flying backwards, away from the Super Sucker, back into Queen Smellina's mouth, then popping back out onto the roof and up into the sky. Everything, the whole day, was whizzing backwards. Before I knew it, weeks, months, and years were flashing by. The numbers on the remote's current date counter counted backwards, earlier and earlier. Then the remote was just a blur of color and light. And heat. Lots of heat. I closed my eyes.

The remote was glowing red hot, but I held on tight and pressed Pause.

Everything screeched to a halt.

I opened my eyes
and looked right
into the eyes of a
very hungry
Tyrannosaurus
rex. He was lick-
ing his lips. The
counter read "65
Million B.C." The

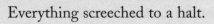

T. rex roared very,
very, very, very loudly.

Oops. I pressed Fast
Forward and left the T. rex in the prehistoric dust.

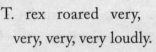

Time flew forward in a flash. A
saber-toothed tiger, a caveman . . . I
think I saw Abe Lincoln. Hard to
tell when you're racing by at thou-
sands of years per second.

I pressed Slow Forward to avoid
going past the present and into the
future.

I Paused to a stop. My thumb was

hurting even more. The remote's counter flashed "Today" and I found myself on the roof of the World Famous Bucket o' Beans All-You-Can-Eat Restaurant. The remote's pieces burst into flames and fell to the rooftop.

Unfortunately, I didn't time my arrival quite right: Blunder Mutt was sticking out of Queen Smellina's mouth and was just about to get spit out—again.

The Super Sucker was teetering on the edge again.

Queen Smellina was arching her back again.

It was all happening *again*!

Queen Smellina hacked Blunder at the Super Sucker.

I leaped with all my might and collided with Blunder in midair, knocking him off course. *Way* off course! He soared over the

ocean, over the horizon . . . and out of sight. Oh, man. I didn't mean for *that* to happen. But now I didn't have the remote to rewind him back.

Granny!

I did a head tuck, a series of high-speed hand-springs, and landed right next to the Super Sucker.

I quickly repro-grammed the Super Sucker and entered Stop Sucking, and then Anti Suck. The machine made a screeching, grinding sound, roared like a very sick ele-phant, and out popped the superheroes.

The Bodacious Backwards Woman was the last to emerge—and clinging to her was the family of squir-rels, now more terrified than angry.

I hugged Granny hard.

She hugged me even harder.

"Partners *always* were we," she said.

I'm a tough superperson. Definitely not a crybaby. But I found myself too choked up to speak.

"Up growing are you now but."

"Yeah."

"Sidekick *own* your need you now so."

"Yeah."

"Superhero own your you're now because."

CHAPTER 22:

Honeymoon over

Just then, I heard a huge, horrible shriek of love.

I turned to see Queen Smellina hugging what she thought was Hunky Valentine. You could tell from the glowing green lip prints on the McButt piñata that she had been smooching it all this time.

And then she shrieked something I didn't expect.

"LUNCHTIME!"

Okay, I'm sure you've heard of the praying mantis (*mantis religiosa*). Well, the shrieking stinkbug (*stinkus shriekatus*) is no relation, but apparently they have one really bad thing in common: Queen Smellina was preparing to eat her mate. She took out a knife, fork, napkin, tablecloth, candles, salt and pepper, and hot sauce. She put on some nice dinner music and opened her mouth very, very, very wide.

But because this particular meal was a police officer, and three or four super roommates, something had to be done. And I had to be the one to do it.

I instantly snapped my head back and then forward, and in one tremendous burst, I unleashed a super-concentrated blast of High-Def Video-Zombie Hypno-Stare power. The scorching blue video ray leaped from my eyes and instantly zombified Queen Smellina. She never knew what hit her.

And what exactly *did* hit her? She was a zombie all right, but what *kind* of zombie?

Well, I can't exactly explain why, but at the precise moment I let loose that ray, a certain old, very irritating TV commercial had popped into my head. It advertised walnuts: sugar-soaked, candy-coated, tooth-filling–removing walnuts. In the ad, a bouncy little walnut guy, with a happy-creepy face and an unbelievably insulting voice, danced and sang an annoying little song. A *really* annoying little song. I had no idea how a Video-Zombie Hypno-Stare infected with this particular image might affect someone, but I didn't have to wait long to find out.

The queen's eyes pulsed with every color of a nauseating rainbow. The rest of her looked as dead as a dead fish. And then, *snap!* She jumped up. Her face twisted into a sickeningly

sweet expression. Her huge smile looked exactly like that freaky walnut character from long ago. And, to everyone's amazement, Queen Smellina, the Shrieking Stinkbug of Stench, started dancing and singing:

"Ohhhhhhhhhhh . . .
I'm Wally, Wally Nutt,
If you're hungry, tell you what,
Crack my shell and shout
hooray,
Eat a Wally Nutt today!"

It was a simple jingle, not much to it, really. But its true horror came from the fact that this Wally idiot would sing it over and over with the same creepy smile and pound the jingle into your brain. Every time that "Ohhhhhh!" came around, you felt as if you might go insane. If you heard the song once, you'd sing it for weeks. And you'd find yourself chomping Wally Nutts for breakfast, lunch, and dinner.

So, anyway, Queen Smellina kept repeating it, a little faster each time.

For the full effect, try smiling like a crazy stinkbug

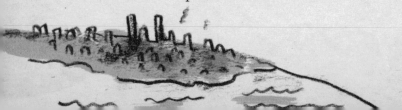

acting like a crazy walnut, and sing the jingle yourself. Over and over and over.

As effective as that old TV ad was on kids, it was ten times more effective on a certain family of squirrels. Who hadn't eaten all day. They started chasing Queen Smellina 'round and 'round the rooftop, like hounds after a rabbit.

Then I remembered that we were all still hovering high above Gritty City, the whole building hanging under the Fabian blimp, and I had no idea how the heck we'd get back down.

The superhero roommates huddled up.

Wonder Boulder, Super Vacation Man, SuperSass CuteGirl, Pooky the Paranormal Parakeet, and the Frankenstein Punster all crammed inside Mighty Tighty Whitey, who hammered in a nail to hook his head/waistband on the roof. The Impossibly Tough Two-Headed Infant got in last, removed a diaper pin, and held it out in front. Then

Mighty Tighty Whitey leaped over the side.

They bungee-jumped way, way down. They were gone a long time.

I started to worry.

But then they came flying back up toward the big fat blimp named Fabian.

And then I *really* worried.

I hit the deck. *"It's gonna blow!"*

They slammed into the blimp.

It didn't blow.

That super two-headed baby sure has a super way with a diaper pin. It made a teeny hole, just big enough to cause a tiny jet of stinky air to shoot out, making a high-pitched farting sound and zigzagging the building and all of us across the sky.

We zipped around for a while until Fabian started running low on gas. Then Super Vacation Man used his super hang-gliding skills to crash-land us into the exercise yard of the Gritty City Jail.

The landing broke open the piñata and Sergeant Bub McButt immediately arrested Granny. "I'm sure you don't have a license to drive a flatulent blimp, you backwards woman I've never met before."

Wonder Boulder leaped into action, knocking McButt on his butt and sitting on his chest. SuperSass threatened him with a super-permanent makeover in pink-and-lavender flowers and polka dots. The Frankenstein Punster pummeled him with puns, ending with this one: "IF YOU'RE AMERI-

CAN WHEN GO *IN* BATHROOM AND YOU'RE AMERICAN WHEN COME *OUT* BATHROOM," the Punster said, "WHAT ARE YOU WHILE *IN* BATHROOM?" and before Pooky or anyone else could say a thing, he shouted, "EUROPEAN!"

McButt dropped the charges.

Granny thanked him. "With worked ever I've piñata undercover superest the far by are you!"

He looked confused, then happy.

Queen Smellina and Fabian were thrown into the slammer. I reminded the nice prison people to lock the locks *before* throwing away the keys this time.

CHAPTER 23:
Home is where the
Many weird superheroes are

We all crammed into the Backwardsmobile and got to know each other a lot better in the process. It took eight seconds to get home. (The extra load really slowed us down.) There was a huge pile of new trophies waiting for us on the porch.

Granny had Tasmanian eel soup and sandwiches delivered and I paid for it with some trophies. It was actually nice to share a meal with those crazy kooks. It turns out that all the roommates have other talents we haven't seen in action yet. The twins do something involving their diaper, which I'd rather not talk about, but it's definitely a super-potent power. Wonder Boulder can break himself up into a tiny army using something called Hyper-Gravelization. Pooky thought a long list of her superpowers to us and blew all our minds. Super Vacation Man described something called Super Time-Sharing, which means that—subject to some restrictions—he can be in two places at once.

"Gee, SVM, that might have come in handy today," I said.

"It only works—*vroom, splash, splash*—every third weekend," he replied. "Neither of me ever gets a vacation out of it, though."

My very bodacious grandmother jumped onto the table and sang the Gettysburg Address backwards to the tune of "You Ain't Nothin' But a Hound Dog." We laughed 'til our faces and stomachs hurt. Then she sang it in Pig Latin, also backwards, and we laughed 'til our eyeballs hurt.

But we all got sad when we thought about old Blunder Mutt. He was by far the stupidest mutt we'd ever met, but also a very good dog. We drank a toast to him with maraschino cherry juice on the rocks—real rocks—his favorite.

Super Vacation Man was the saddest. He blew his nose: *"Honk!"* His voice cracked as he said, "Ahhh, Blunder Mutt. He reminded me of another mutt—*woof, woof.* The mutt I had when I was but a pup—*whimper-whimper.* Not a day goes by—*zip, whiz, bye-bye*—that I don't think of my sweet little Scoodlyboot. And just think, now Blunder and Scoodly are frolicking together in that dog park in the sky. Runnin' side-by-side, panting away—*heh-heh*—tongues hangin' out—*slobber-slobber*—on a forever stretch o' beach, chasin' flyin' squirrels and angels and other heavenly critters—*tweet-tweet, chitter-chitter, squawk-squawk!*—gettin' all wet n' sandy. . . .

Oh, I love it when they get that way, even if the super station wagon does get all messy. Well, anyhoo . . . he was a good dog, and he's gone to where the good doggies go—*sniffle, sniffle, WAHHH!*—and we'll never see ol' Blunder again. Never, ever, ever, ever, ever. Ever."

Just then, we heard a loud gurgling sound coming from the lair. We got there just as the sink exploded, depositing Blunder Mutt and about a hundred gallons

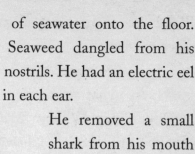

of seawater onto the floor. Seaweed dangled from his nostrils. He had an electric eel in each ear.

He removed a small shark from his mouth and smiled. "Homely, sweet homely!"

Everyone cheered.

Super Vacation Man was superhappy to see Blunder, and Blunder was even happier to see him. The mutt jumped for joy until SVM rubbed his belly.

Blunder looked up at me. He spoke slowly, like he was speaking to an idiot. "Maybe next time you try use you brainy a little smartisher," he said, pointing to his head. "If you jesta call ol'

Blundy-boy soonisher, you wouldn't a getted in so much troubles!"

I decided to ignore that.

"Guess what, Amazing Techno Bloke," said Mighty Tighty Whitey. "We all 'elped grandmum bake you a tin of Super-Chew Choco-Chunk Crusty-Crunches for dessert!"

I was touched. Maybe this was what it was like to be part of a big family.

"Guess what else?" said Biff and Smiff, picking their tooth. "We just ate 'em. A growing, muscle-bound double baby must consume seventy-four times his/their body weight each day, and that's a fact. Actually, we just made that up . . . but we were really hungry, and *that* is a fact."

I was about to say that I officially hated room-mates, when I noticed that the phone had been ringing for a superlong time.

"Gee," I said, "might there be an official phone answerer in the house?"

CHAPTER 24:

One Last Chapter, Leading to More Chapters

Blunder blew a gasket: "No! I sorry! I not the fone-answer-fish no more! It always them wrongish numbers. It gotta be that same what's-his-facey what called sixty-two times already for Super Vacationy Man. Somethin' 'bout Demented ringwormers of Fire or such sillybillyness. I don't know . . . ice caps boiling . . . ends of world . . . blah, blah, blah . . ."

Super Vacation Man dived across the room and answered the phone.

"House of super weirdos! Super Vacation Man speaking!" He listened for a second and slammed it back down, saying, *"Slam!"*

"Blunder, you good mutt, you," he said. "You were right, it was that very same what's-his-name."

"I know!" Blunder laughed uncontrollably. "He be such a foolishy kookoohead!"

"Yes, but I think Mayor What's-His-Name might actually be serious about that whole—*sizzle, kaboom, fizzle*—end of the world thing," said Super Vacation Man. "I was hoping to take some time off, but what the heck . . ."

He posed heroically, put his hands together over his head like a high diver, and called in a booming, super catchphrasey sort of way, *"There . . . goes . . . my . . . vacation!"* And he dived through one of the Wonder Boulder-shaped holes in the wall and into the Gritty City night.

We could hear him complaining in the distance: "You'd think if a superhero never got a vacation, he'd at least get a sidekick!"

Blunder Mutt's eyes bugged out and he fell flat on his face. He popped up like an insane jack-in-the-box. "Yes, yes, yessy-yes, Man of Vacationeers! I can kick sides with the bestest of them and I'm a-comin' too!"

But then he stopped in his tracks. "Oh, but no! Me 'member now. Me already be kickin' sides fer a people who *need* help, a *lotta* help, and me be loyalty to this royalty named . . . Amazey Duke o' Tacky No!"

I did still want a sidekick, but he wasn't it. "Thanks, Blunder, but you and SVM make a darn good team. One of the classics. You go ahead, I'll be fine. I'll find someone else to kick my sides."

Blunder Mutt hugged me so hard I thought I'd lose my dinner. He put his head down, tail up, lunged forward, tripped over Wonder Boulder, and crashed a new hole through the wall, shouting, *"Whole wide worldy, hear me call . . . Blunder Nut be save you all!"*

We all said good-bye to the mutt except one of us, who cheerfully shouted, *"Luck . . . good!"*

AFTERWARDS

At exactly 3:32 A.M. I was awakened by a loud knocking. I opened the door and almost stepped on a small creature. The face was familiar, but he was wearing a cape, a ten-gallon hat, and a pair of blinking space boots. He was smaller than Pooky. He must have followed me home and somehow got shrunken and mixed up by a few wrong turns while traveling through time.

"Super Teeny Tiny Tyrannosaurus Tex 3000 at your service!" He smiled, baring a mouthful of glowing green metallic teeth. He flicked his bright orange tongue, sparks crackling off the tip. Then he chomped down on my ankle and didn't let go. I limped back into the house, dragging along the growling space cowboy dinosaur who was gripping my leg like a very small, very insane poodle.

"Granny's gonna love you," I said.

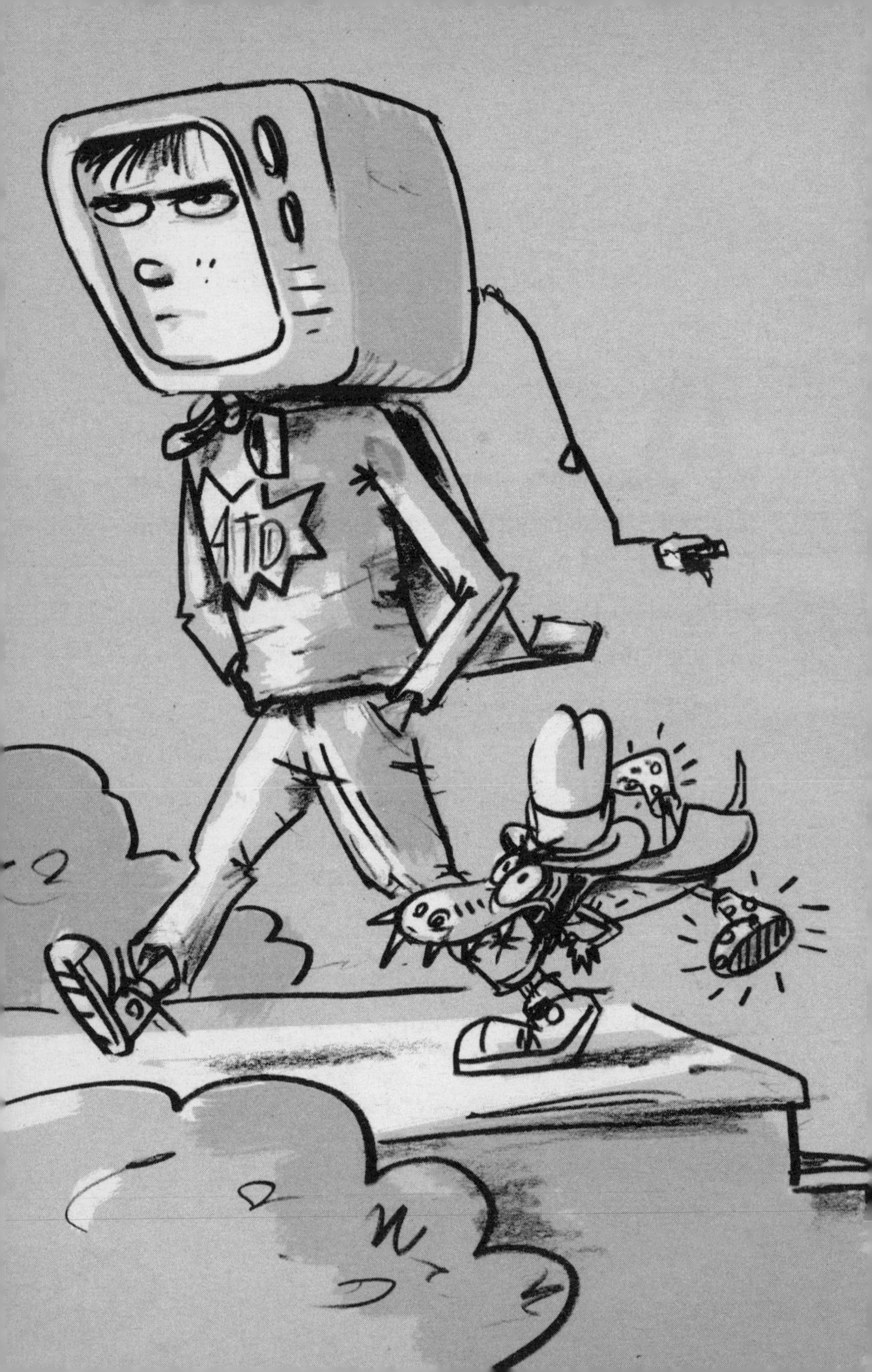
ATD

there are more goofy adventures
ahead for the super-roommates in

SUPER GOOFBALLS #2
Goofballs in paradise

The Big Contest

Back at the house, the phone rang for a long time before I remembered that Blunder Mutt was gone and no one else was going to answer it.

"House of Super Goofballs, Amazing Techno Dude speaking."

"Good morning, Mayor What's-His-Name speaking. And speaking of speaking, may I speak to Super Vacation Man?"

"He left hours ago."

"Hmmmm. That's funny. Actually, it's not funny. Completely unfunny. He was supposed to come to Gritty City City Hall, so I could tell him about an important case, and he hasn't shown up yet. I talked to that lunatic Blunder Mutt sixteen times. Did he give him the message?"

"Well, sort of. But you also talked to SVM on the phone last night, right?"

"Wrong."

"I was standing right next to him. He said, 'Hello, Mayor What's-His-Name! Yes, Mayor What's-His-Name! *Blam-bing-whammo*, Mayor What's-His-Name!"

"Well, maybe he was talking to some *other* Mayor What's-His-Name."

That seemed unlikely. Something was fishy here. Where the heck had SVM and Blunder Mutt gone? Were they okay?

"Frankly, my dude, I don't give a darn," said the mayor. "Tell you what. This was the perfect job for Super Vacation Man, but I'm calling on you to save the day instead. And the day is definitely in need of saving!"

"I'll be there in two sec-onds!"

"It can't wait that long. I'll tell you over the phone.

That supervillain sourpuss Mondo Grumpo, is on the move, plotting something very grumpy."

"Sounds like a pain in the you-know-what, but grumpy is not exactly *evil*."

"This is no ordinary grumpiness! This is super *evil* grumpiness!"

"It can't be too evil. I've barely even *heard* of Mondo Grumpo. He's not even on the Slimy Sleazeball Superchart."

"Wrong. While you were busy sniffing out Queen Smellina the Shrieking Stinkbug of Stench, the rest of the evil world didn't just stop being evil, you know! Mondo Grumpo hit the superchart last week and moved up fast. In fact, he was number two until you threw Queen Smellina into jail. So, now he's . . ."

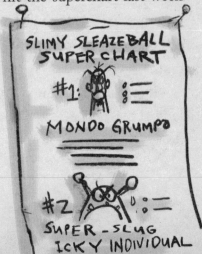

SLIMY SLEAZEBALL SUPER CHART

#1:

MONDO GRUMPO

#2

SUPER-SLUG
ICKY INDIVIDUAL

"Number *one* on the Slimy Sleazeball Superchart?!"

"Wow, you are good at math. Anyway, Mondo Grumpo is anti-fun of any kind. He never laughs. Never smiles. His superpowers are super grumpiness and negativity. He uses a super scolding technique called 'The Evil Finger Shake of Shame.' He shakes his finger and negative lightning bolts shoot from his fingertip. This, together with his horrifying, super-grumpy frown, delivers a deadly dose of disapproval. It makes his victims feel really, really bad. Even if you've done nothing wrong, you feel like your teacher has caught you cheating on a test . . . and you're in your underwear . . . and your underwear's full of holes . . . and the whole classroom, no, the whole *world*, is

HA! HA! HA! HA! HA! HA! HA!

laughing at you. Only a million times worse. What would happen if he ever found out a way to do the Evil Finger Shake of Shame to the whole world?"

"Let me guess: every bit of fun in the world would be gone?"

"Wow, you are supersmart. I guess that's why you're a cool superdude."

"Being mayor is pretty cool, too."

"You think so? Today I have an all-day meeting with fifteen boring people making boring speeches. Every time I fall asleep, they poke me with pencils to wake me up and then start their boring speeches from the beginning again. You wanna trade places?"

"Well, no. I guess not."

"Okay, then, get going! Right away! Sooner if possible!"

check out the first two silly, outrageously funny books in the Super Goofballs series!

Super Goofballs, Book 1: That Stinking Feeling

Amazing Techno Dude and his grandmother, the Bodacious Backwards Woman, are forced to take in roommates to cover expenses—which is how they end up with a house full of wacky, little-known superheroes, including Blunder Mutt, the Frankenstein Punster, the Impossibly Tough Two-Headed Infant, and Pooky the Paranormal Parakeet (to name just a few!). Living with a bunch of super goofballs is challenging enough, but when it's also your job to save the world from crazy, smelly supervillains, what's one kid (with a TV for a head) supposed to do?

Super Goofballs, Book 2: Goofballs in Paradise

The hilarious adventures continue as Super Vacation Man, along with his new sidekick, Blunder Mutt, blasts off in pursuit of a dastardly do-badder named Mondo Grumpo. Or is that really where Super Vacation Man went? When Amazing Techno Dude discovers that this roommate has secretly snuck off for a resort vacation, he realizes it's up to him to track down Mondo Grumpo and save the world (again). Meanwhile, the other roommates squabble over who gets to be his sidekick…and Blunder Mutt (disguised as a potted plant) blunders into terrible, terrible danger!